"Don't cry, Rina," Hunter whispered.

"Remember, this is not about what we want, but about what's best for young Billy."

Rina lifted her eyes, stunned by how close Hunter was and how much he was affecting her.

He agreed with the Tribal law, agreed that she shouldn't be allowed to raise her orphaned nephew. So how could she be responding to him like this? How could she feel so many emotions racing through her, angering her, exciting her?

The warmth of his body, the heat of his hands was wreaking havoc on her. In spite of her anger, her pain, she knew from the look in Hunter's eyes what he wanted to do…what she longed for him to do.

"We…can't…do…this. We—"

But his mouth stopped her words, and desire flared so hot, so quickly, she was certain it would incinerate them both….

Dear Reader,

Happy 20ᵗʰ Anniversary, Silhouette! And Happy Valentine's Day to all! There are so many ways to celebrate…starting with six spectacular novels this month from Special Edition.

Reader favorite Joan Elliott Pickart concludes Silhouette's exciting cross-line continuity ROYALLY WED with *Man…Mercenary… Monarch,* in which a beautiful woman challenges a long-lost prince to give up his loner ways.

In *Dr. Mom and the Millionaire,* Christine Flynn's latest contribution to the popular series PRESCRIPTION: MARRIAGE, a marriage-shy tycoon suddenly experiences a sizzling attraction—to his gorgeous doctor! And don't miss the next SO MANY BABIES—in *Who's That Baby?* by Diana Whitney, an infant girl is left on a Native American attorney's doorstep, and he turns to a lovely pediatrician for help.…

Next is Lois Faye Dyer's riveting *Cattleman's Courtship,* in which a brooding, hard-hearted rancher is undeniably drawn to a chaste, sophisticated lady. And in Sharon De Vita's provocative family saga, THE BLACKWELL BROTHERS, tempers—and passions— flare when a handsome Apache man offers *The Marriage Basket* to a captivating city gal.

Finally, you'll be swept up in the drama of Trisha Alexander's *Falling for an Older Man,* another tale in the CALLAHANS & KIN series, when an unexpected night of passion leaves Sheila Callahan with a nine-month secret.

So, curl up with a Special Edition novel and celebrate this Valentine's Day with thoughts of love and happy dreams of forever!

Happy reading,

Karen Taylor Richman,
Senior Editor

Please address questions and book requests to:
Silhouette Reader Service
U.S.: 3010 Walden Ave., P.O. Box 1325, Buffalo, NY 14269
Canadian: P.O. Box 609, Fort Erie, Ont. L2A 5X3

SHARON DE VITA

THE MARRIAGE BASKET

Silhouette®

SPECIAL EDITION®

Published by Silhouette Books

America's Publisher of Contemporary Romance

The author gratefully acknowledges and thanks artist
Carol A. Douglas, whose hand-crafted Marriage Basket
helped inspire this book.

SILHOUETTE BOOKS

ISBN 0-373-24307-3

THE MARRIAGE BASKET

Visit us at www.romance.net

Printed in U.S.A.

Books by Sharon De Vita

Silhouette Special Edition

Child of Midnight #1013
*The Lone Ranger #1078
*The Lady and the Sheriff #1103
*All It Takes Is Family #1126
†The Marriage Basket #1307

*Silver Creek County
†The Blackwell Brothers
**Lullabies and Love

Silhouette Romance

Heavenly Match #475
Lady and the Legend #498
Kane and Mabel #545
Baby Makes Three #573
Sherlock's Home #593
Italian Knights #610
Sweet Adeline #693
**On Baby Patrol #1276
**Baby with a Badge #1298
**Baby and the Officer #1316

SHARON DE VITA

is a *USA Today* bestselling, award-winning author of numerous works of fiction and nonfiction. Her first novel won a national writing competition for Best Unpublished Romance Novel of 1985. This award-winning book, *Heavenly Match,* was subsequently published by Silhouette in 1986.

A frequent guest speaker and lecturer at conferences and seminars across the country, Sharon is currently an Adjunct Professor of Literature and Communications at a private college in the Midwest. With over one million copies of her novels in print, Sharon's professional credentials have earned her a place in *Who's Who in American Authors, Editors and Poets* as well as the *International Who's Who of Authors.* In 1987, Sharon was the proud recipient of *Romantic Times Magazine*'s Lifetime Achievement Award for Excellence in Writing.

She currently makes her home in a small suburb of Chicago, with her two college-age daughters and her teenage son.

IT'S OUR 20th ANNIVERSARY!
We'll be celebrating all year, continuing with these fabulous titles, on sale in February 2000.

Special Edition

#1303 Man...Mercenary... Monarch
Joan Elliott Pickart

#1304 Dr. Mom and the Millionaire
Christine Flynn

#1305 Who's That Baby?
Diana Whitney

#1306 Cattleman's Courtship
Lois Faye Dyer

#1307 The Marriage Basket
Sharon De Vita

#1308 Falling for an Older Man
Trisha Alexander

Intimate Moments

#985 The Wildes of Wyoming–Chance
Ruth Langan

#986 Wild Ways
Naomi Horton

#987 Mistaken Identity
Merline Lovelace

#988 Family on the Run
Margaret Watson

#989 On Dangerous Ground
Maggie Price

#990 Catch Me If You Can
Nina Bruhns

Romance

#1426 Waiting for the Wedding
Carla Cassidy

#1427 Bringing Up Babies
Susan Meier

#1428 The Family Diamond
Moyra Tarling

#1429 Simon Says...Marry Me!
Myrna Mackenzie

#1430 The Double Heart Ranch
Leanna Wilson

#1431 If the Ring Fits...
Melissa McClone

Desire

#1273 A Bride for Jackson Powers
Dixie Browning

#1274 Sheikh's Temptation
Alexandra Sellers

#1275 The Daddy Salute
Maureen Child

#1276 Husband for Keeps
Kate Little

#1277 The Magnificent M.D.
Carol Grace

#1278 Jesse Hawk: Brave Father
Sheri WhiteFeather

Prologue

She found him cowering in a ball in a corner of the front porch. Startled, Emma Blackwell almost dropped the empty egg basket as her gaze took in the little boy of about five.

His face was badly bruised and his hair, which was tangled with bramble and brush, hung nearly to his shoulders. His clothing was nearly threadbare and hung off his far too skinny frame which was dotted with an assortment of bruises in a rainbow of colors from light yellow to deep purple.

Instinctively, Emma started toward him, to comfort, to soothe, then froze as he recoiled in obvious fear.

Tears filled her eyes. She'd never seen a child in such pitiful condition before, and it immediately tore at her heart.

"Justin?" Clutching the egg basket in her hands, Emma tried to keep the panic out of her voice as she called to her husband. "Justin, you'd better come out here. Now."

"Emma?" Frowning, Justin pushed open the screen door, his face still full of shaving cream, a bath towel tossed carelessly over his bare shoulder. "What's the—" He saw the child then, and for a moment he, too, stared in stunned surprise. "Oh, Lord," he said softly. His heart nearly broke at the sight of the child. He'd been beaten, there was no doubt about it.

Justin's fists clenched. Memories of his own pathetic childhood, when he'd been abandoned, then sentenced to life in a children's home, where he'd been beaten regularly for even the mildest infraction swept over him, and he swore again.

Their animals were in better condition than this child, Justin thought. The poor little thing was little more than bruised, battered flesh hanging over bones.

Justin turned toward Emma, saw the look of love and longing in her eyes and swallowed the lump that had lodged in his throat.

No one would ever know the gut-wrenching disappointment they'd felt, the long hours in the dark of night, when they'd held each other and cried, grieving for the children they'd never raise; the babies they'd never conceive.

Their love was so huge, so all encompassing, it

just didn't seem fair. They had so much to give and no one to give it to.

He'd escaped the poverty and shame of his youth, vowing to make something of himself, and he had. At eighteen, with not even a name of his own, he'd lit out of the children's home, taken the name of this town—Blackwell—and made it his home. His first real home.

Then he'd met Emma. His beautiful, loving Emma. It was the final piece of the puzzle. Together they'd worked to build a life, a future.

Now, he had Emma and all the riches anyone could ever want, but none of it meant anything without a child to fill their hearts or their home.

"Justin." Emma looked at him, laying a hand on his bare arm. "We have to do something." She started toward the child, but Justin caught her hand.

"He's scared, honey," he said quietly. "Be careful." He knew what a scared, frightened, cornered child was capable of.

"Where do you think he came from?"

"I don't know." Frowning, Justin looked at the child more closely. "Looks like he's part Indian. Probably Apache." Justin turned toward the east. "There's a Lipan reservation not far from here, one of the last Apache reservations in Texas." His eyes narrowed. "It might be worth a visit."

"He's just a baby," Emma whispered, as she moved slowly closer. The little bundle of boy with the wide dark eyes cowered farther in the corner. Trying not to frighten him more, Emma went down on her knees until she was eye level with him. "Hello, sweetheart," she crooned, instinctively brushing the sleek, tangle of black hair off his battered face with a gentle, loving hand. "Don't be afraid," Emma cooed. "No one's going to hurt you."

Gently, she pulled his frail body close, engulfing him in her arms, before turning her head toward Justin, her eyes glinting in determination.

"Honey, run inside and tell Sadie to run a nice hot bath," she instructed, her mind already whirling. "Then have her make up one of the spare bedrooms."

The house had six bedrooms, bedrooms they'd planned to fill with children. Bedrooms that had stayed empty. Until now.

Emma stroked the child's head, drawing back to look at him. She smiled tenderly. "Are you hungry?" She laughed suddenly. "How silly. Of course you're hungry, little boys are always hungry." She took his trembling hand, then drew him to his feet as she rose. Slowly, she started across the porch. "What's your name, sweetheart?"

"Hun...ter," he whispered, clutching Emma's hand like a lifeline. Emma grinned, her empty maternal heart suddenly overflowing with love.

"Hunter. Why, that's a wonderful name, son."
Son.

Justin caught Emma's reverently whispered word, a word filled with such hope, such longing it made his heart ache.

His gaze shifted from Emma to the battered, frightened child, and he felt something warm wrap tightly around his guarded heart.

Son.

"Justin?" Turning to him, Emma paused on the porch, a silent pleading question in her voice, in her heart.

Justin's smile was slow and glorious. "Emma, honey, how about right after breakfast I take a ride over to the reservation and see if I can find out anything." He reached for her other hand, wanting to close the distance between the three of them, to form a protective shield that would protect them all against the harsh cruelties of the world.

At least their world.

His gaze shifted to the child, standing there helplessly looking up at him and Emma with such...hope, such trust.

Justin's jaw tightened. He'd be damned if he'd ever let anyone take or hurt this helpless little boy. Not ever again. He'd been there too many times himself.

Nor would he let anyone destroy the joy he saw in Emma's eyes, and in her heart. He'd waited too long for this moment, too long to see the emptiness in Emma's eyes gone, filled with a mother's love.

"I think Hunter's a real fine name." Moving carefully, Justin reached for the child's other hand.

With eyes wide and wary, the little boy glanced up at him and a soft, slow smile finally curved his swollen lips.

The empty place Justin had carried deep inside him for so many years, filled.

"Hunter Blackwell," Justin said softly, swinging the little guy up and holding him protectively in his arms. The boy was as light and frail as a feather. "Welcome home."

Justin's voice caught as the child's skinny battered arms slowly, hesitantly, trustingly looped around his neck, and he laid his weary head on Justin's wide shoulder. "Welcome home, son."

Chapter One

Blackwell, Texas
Twenty-five years later

He hadn't been able to sleep.

Sometime during the night the hoot of the owl had awakened him, sending chills through him, for he knew that something was wrong.

Before the sun rose to spill light over the horizon, Dr. Hunter Blackwell had showered and dressed, and was now heading for the small tribal clinic where he saw patients every morning.

Even in the predawn Texas morning, the air was hot and sticky. A breeze occasionally fluttered, but it felt like a blast from a hot furnace, giving no relief.

The waiting room was already full when he arrived. Beth Anne, his very efficient nurse, began ushering mothers and children in, trying to keep order among the chaos and crying.

This morning, Hunter found the chaos and the crying soothing. Life signs, he thought as he tried to keep up with the steady stream of patients, knowing that keeping busy was a way to calm his inner turmoil.

It was almost noon when Beth Anne came bursting into an examining room just as he was finishing an inoculation of a rather rambunctious toddler.

"He's here," Beth Anne announced without preamble or apology, wringing her hands.

Hunter didn't bother to look up. Beth Anne had a flair for dramatics, but she was the best pediatric nurse he'd ever had. Which was why he overlooked her obvious rudeness.

But she was white and had no understanding of the Life-Ways of The People or how important peace was, so he excused her frequent bouts and bursts.

"Hunter, did you hear me?" She stepped closer, eyes wide, hands still wringing like a too wet mop.

"I heard you," he said gently, pulling up the screaming toddler's diaper, before scooping the child into his arms.

He rocked the boy gently, whispering softly, rubbing his large hand down the child's back until he quieted.

Still holding the child, Hunter reached into a clear

glass jar on the table and handed the baby a sugar-less lollipop. Content now, the child grinned, proudly showing several small teeth as Hunter transferred him into his waiting mother's arms.

Hunter waited until mother and baby were safely out of the room, having to sidestep around Beth Anne to go on their way. Finally, he turned his attention to her.

"*Who* is here, Beth Anne?" he said with the infinite patience he was known for.

Her eyes darted about, this way and that. "That…that…man."

Hunter nodded slowly, banking down a smile. "I see." He didn't particularly see anything at the moment, except that something, or rather someone, had flustered her. "And which man would that be?" he asked, turning to the sink to wash his hands.

"You know…that man. Your…" She seemed to search for a word. "Your…grandfather," she said, not quite sure she had the right word but settling for it anyway. "Mr. Dinyen."

Hunter slowly straightened, shutting off the water and reaching for one of the disposable towels. Carefully he dried his hands before turning to her.

"The Din-yen is here?" he asked in surprise. It was rare for the Wise One to leave his sacred place on the reservation, especially now that age had bowed his legs and bent his body.

The Din-yen, or Shaman, was called the Wise One. He was the elder of the tribe, and the wisest of the wise. He had inherited his powers as a youth, and looked forward to passing on his powers to his young grandson, Billy. There was no greater honor among The People.

Absently, Hunter touched the small brown leather pouch he wore around his neck; it was filled with the potent power of *ha-dintin,* the pollen of tule cattails, believed by The People to protect against the Spirits of Evil and Mischief. The Shaman had given it to Hunter when he was just a small boy and he had worn it ever since. Hunter frowned. If the Wise One was here, at the clinic, then it had to be something of importance. The Shaman rarely left the reservation anymore.

Hunter inhaled a slow breath, held it for a moment, then expelled it slowly, as if trying to expel the unease that had walked with him since he'd first heard the hoot of the owl during the darkness of last night.

"Where is he?" he asked, glancing at his nurse.

Beth Anne swallowed hard, still wringing her hands. "In your office. I asked him…to wait in your office."

"Thank you, Beth Anne." Hunter tossed the used towels in the plastic-lined basket, then headed down the hall toward his back office.

He paused for a moment, not wanting to intrude. The door was open, and the Wise One stood with his back to him, leaning heavily on his walking stick, staring out the window. He didn't need to turn around to sense Hunter's presence.

"I have come to ask a favor," the old man said quietly, still staring out the window.

"Anything," Hunter said to the man who meant so much to him. A man who had befriended a little half-breed boy who had no family of his own; a man who had taken him into his heart after he'd been adopted by the Blackwells, and taught him the Holy-Life Way of The People; a man who had helped him to understand not just who he was, but where he belonged in this great space of the universe.

He loved the Wise One just as he loved Justin Blackwell, his father. The father who had not sired him, but had raised and loved him just the same, helping him to understand the ways of *his* life.

Together, their knowledge had blended and flowed through Hunter, teaching him, training him, helping him to find his rightful place in both worlds. It hadn't always been an easy journey. At times, it was still difficult, straddling two different worlds when he was only one man.

But he kept trying, day by day, hoping to be worthy of the love both men—his fathers—had shared and given to him.

"The Death Spirit visited my family last night."

Hunter stepped closer, suddenly understanding the unease that had dogged him for hours; the hooting of the owl in the darkness of night. His thoughts immediately went to the Wise One's grandchild, and Hunter's godson. "Billy?"

The Wise One turned, his movements slow and

obviously painful. Leaning heavily on his walking stick, he looked old and frail. He smiled slowly.

"No, my grandson is well." His smile faded a bit. "It is the boy's mother, my daughter and her husband. The Death Spirit found them during the moon's time last night."

Hunter wouldn't allow himself to feel. He couldn't. Not yet. He would remember fondly Jane Eaglefeather and her husband, James, two people who had honored him with their friendship.

James had come to the reservation to teach, but it was he who had learned, about the Holy-Life Way, and about The People and he'd stayed, making his home among them.

Hunter had made a solemn promise to Jane and her husband on the day he helped deliver their only child, Billy. If anything ever happened to them, he would step in and teach and guide the boy in the Holy-Life Way of The People, just as the Wise One had once guided him.

He thought of the boy now, barely fourteen, and a million questions popped into Hunter's head.

The Apache in him knew that to ask questions that were not his business was not the Life-Way, and yet the doctor in him, the healer ached for the boy who would feel lost, abandoned, and above all alone.

He knew, because he'd been there.

Hunter suppressed a sigh. It was hard enough for a young boy to grow into manhood, but when one had to shoulder the burden of a loss this heavy, as well as the knowledge that he had sacred steps to fill in the future, life could be a painful journey, especially when that boy had a foot in two cultures.

Hunter finally let loose a quiet sigh.

This was one of those times when he felt the weight of his dual lives.

Now he understood the owl's hoot he heard last night. It was the Death Spirit passing over the child, to touch his parents.

"My grandson needs to be told that his mother and father are now one with the universe." Hunter merely nodded, waiting for the old man to continue. "I will take him to the mouth of the canyon, to my summer hogan, so he can be one with nature, so he will be able to understand that his parents are now also one with the universe."

"I understand."

"This favor I ask will not be easy." The old man glanced down at his hands for a moment, then lifted his gaze to Hunter's. "I have come to you because you have always been wise for your years and because of the special relationship between you and the boy." The old man paused. "And because you as no one else understand their ways."

Their ways?

The words hung in the air for a moment. Hunter felt the first fluttering of panic, but wisely remained silent, letting the Wise One continue.

"There is a woman. She is the sister of the boy's father." The old man gave another sigh, looking off into the distance again. "She does not understand

The Life-Way, or The People. She is the boy's aunt, but she is not one of us." The Wise One took a deep breath, lifting a hand to his chest as the breath wheezed out of him, drifting into a hacking cough.

Hunter went to him, catching him just as his knees buckled, lowering him gently into a chair, kneeling close beside him. He said nothing, merely waiting until the old man had recovered enough to speak.

"I have much to teach the boy before he is ready to accept his rightful place among The People." The old man's voice was thin and raspy. He reached for Hunter's hand. "In three days, this woman, this aunt of the boy, Rina Roberts is coming to see me about the boy's future." The old man began coughing, and Hunter waited, still holding the man's hand, surreptitiously taking his pulse. It was fast, and weak, worrying him.

"She wants to take the boy, to raise him as hers. Explain to her in your white man's words the boy's sacred place among The People." The old man's voice was barely a whisper as he leaned closer. "Tell her…tell her that an Apache child belongs to his mother's people. The boy now belongs to us. He has her blood, yes, but he is one of us." The Wise One laid a hand to his heart. "The People need my grandson to guide them, to use his wisdom to show them the way. I do not understand the white man's world or their ways. But you do, my son. You can make her understand."

Weary now, the old man leaned back against the chair and closed his eyes. "Will you do this for me, my great friend?'' His eyes opened, but he was too weary to lift his head.

''I will do this,'' Hunter said softly, not knowing *how* he was going to do it, only knowing that he could not deny the Wise One anything.

For a moment, his past history rose up to mock him. His dealings with white women in the past had not left him favorably disposed toward them. But not just white women—*any* women, he mentally corrected.

His birth mother had been white, and she'd beaten and abandoned him because she couldn't handle raising a half-breed child, a child who didn't fit in her white world.

You'd think he'd have learned his lesson.

He hadn't.

In medical school, he had the misfortune to fall in love—with another med student. Meagan was different, he told himself. Not like his mother.

Just like his mother, he reminded himself now, already hardening his heart toward this new woman who would come to complicate their lives. Meagan had left him at the altar—accepting a bribe from her father not to marry a half-breed.

His history with women was fatally flawed, teaching him painful lessons about women and their motives and integrity.

His past experiences had been unbearably painful, lessons he would not soon forget.

The Wise One struggled for breath. ''Tell her...tell this white woman...she may not have the boy, nor will we allow her to ever take him from the reservation, from The People.'' The Shaman's eyes searched Hunter's. "Do you understand? Billy belongs to us. Regardless of her blood that runs through the boy's veins, he is one of us. And here he must stay. Do you understand?''

''I understand,'' Hunter said with a nod of his dark head. Now, all he had to do was figure out how he was going to make the child's aunt, Rina Roberts, understand.

Three days later, exhausted after spending the night at the reservation, tending to a child with a rather nasty bout of pneumonia, Hunter arrived at the airport a few minutes late and immediately asked the courtesy desk to page Rina Roberts, fearing he'd missed her.

Leaning against the desk, ignoring the blatant flirting of the young clerk, Hunter kept a watchful eye out for Rina.

He spotted her the moment she walked through the terminal. Although they'd never met, he knew a bit about her because of James. He hadn't needed to meet the woman in person to recognize her.

There was something about her, something he instinctively recognized. Perhaps it was the hair, he reasoned. It was the same wild, vibrant red as her brother's.

Behind his mirrored sunglasses, Hunter observed her trying to nudge her way through the crowded terminal.

She was a small, delicate-looking woman with huge, wary eyes and a cap of vibrant—and, at the moment—unruly red hair that had once been caught up in some kind of topknot, but now had come loose to tumble down, framing the fragile features of her beautiful face.

Her skin was as pale and delicate as a white lily blooming against the background of the dull, drab desert.

She wore a sturdy suit in a serious shade of navy that was clearly not meant for the intense heat and humidity of Texas. She looked wrinkled and rumpled, and entirely too vulnerable for his own peace of mind.

The sight of this small, delicate woman who looked like a frightened fish suddenly thrust out of water, raised all his protective instincts and something shifted deep inside him and he felt his initial, instinctive resentment thaw a bit.

Hunter blew out a breath. For the past few days, ever since he'd learned Rina was coming to Texas, and more pointedly, since he'd learned the reason for it, he had tried to harden his resolve, while not letting his natural sympathy for the woman because of her brother's death get the best of him.

It had helped to think of her as an adversary.

Unfortunately, the sight of her had blown his resolve straight to hell. Some adversary, he thought in disgust. She looked about as helpless and harmless as a babe in the woods.

She also looked absolutely terrified.

She had a lot of guts. Burying her brother, then traveling all the way here in an attempt to claim her brother's only child. And if he remembered correctly, Billy was the last of her family now.

Watching her, as she struggled to juggle her overnight case, her briefcase and her purse as she tried to make her way through the crowd of travelers, he searched his mind for every tidbit James had ever told him about his older sister.

Rina was, he believed, like James a schoolteacher. She had also raised her brother after their own parents' deaths within weeks of each other when she was barely seventeen. As far as he knew she had never been married, and had no family of her own. No husband. No children.

Watching her, he instinctively wondered why some guy hadn't snapped her up. She was beautiful, fragile and breathtaking.

Maybe the guys in Chicago suffered from a terminal case of the stupids, he decided. Because from where he was standing, Rina Roberts was definitely, incredibly all woman.

Albeit, an exhausted, weary woman, he thought, but a beautiful woman nevertheless.

He was a physician, comforting came naturally to him, and it was clear this woman was sorely in need of comfort. In less than a week, she'd lost her only brother.

And now, he was going to have to tell her she was going to lose her nephew as well.

Swearing softly under his breath at the guilt that

suddenly felt like a heavy hand on his shoulder, and feeling torn between duty, his own internal fears and his sudden compassion for this woman and her circumstances, Hunter sighed heavily, and waited as she began to thread her way once again through the crowd.

Rina Roberts was certain she'd landed in hell.

Unfortunately, someone had renamed it Texas.

Juggling her overnight case, her briefcase and her purse as well as her own heavy-duty grief, Rina tried to maneuver her way through the line of weary travelers trying to get through the airport.

She glanced around the small, crowded, wall-less facilities with a scowl. Well, at least she thought it was an airport.

She'd never had to deplane right onto an airfield before, nor had she ever seen an airport terminal that had no windows, merely an overhead tin roof.

But as Dr. Hunter Blackwell had explained yesterday when he'd phoned offering to pick her up from the airport, this was the closest airfield to the reservation, although how the man could consider a hundred miles to be close was beyond her.

Since her brother's and his wife's death in a car accident a little over a week ago, all she'd been able to do was think and worry about her young nephew, Billy. At fourteen, he was alone in the world now, except for her, and his aging grandfather.

She'd been relieved to learn that Billy had been

staying in his grandfather's home, not far from the one Billy had shared with his parents.

Although she knew his grandfather was in extremely poor health, until she could work out Billy's custody arrangement, she was grateful Billy was with family, someone who loved him. The less disruption in Billy's life the better.

Still glancing around the crowded airport, Rina blew out a weary breath, praying for a cool breeze.

The heat was unlike anything she'd ever imagined. But, Rina supposed with a sigh, beggars couldn't be choosers. She was just grateful she was finally here.

Stepping out of the surging line of travelers for a moment, Rina dropped everything from her arms, sorely tempted to collapse along with her gear.

She was exhausted. Grief had clogged her head and swollen her eyes, but it was the Texas heat that had robbed her of her strength and breath.

And the lack of food probably hadn't helped. She hadn't been able to swallow a bite since she'd learned of James's death.

Pushing a few damp, straggling strands of hair from her face, Rina swiped her nose with a delicate lacy hanky, pushed up her glasses, and tried to gather her composure.

Her head came up as she heard her name paged, and she smiled, inhaling a slow, albeit hot breath.

She wouldn't have believed this airport could have a paging system.

Tempted to leave her gear where it was, she finally, reluctantly picked it up and trudged toward the desk where she spotted a young woman smiling up at a man who looked about the size of a sequoia tree.

The girl's lashes were flapping like a flag in the breeze, no doubt in an effort to impress the man.

Normally, the girl's obvious flirting would have made Rina smile and wonder if she'd ever been that bold, or that aggressive, never mind that young.

No, never, Rina decided with an amused smile. She'd always been too adult to engage in such youthful fancy. Besides, even if she did know how to aggressively flirt, which she most assuredly did not, sadly, she'd never met a man she felt the need to impress that much.

Still lugging her gear, Rina sidestepped around the tall, well-built man who was the object of the young woman's obvious attention, not wanting to intrude or be rude, but wanting to get to her destination just the same.

She inched forward, until the counter was nearly pressing into her breasts.

"Excuse me," Rina said. Her throat was incredibly dry. "Excuse me," she said more forcefully.

The woman granted her a glance, one filled with irritation, before turning her attention back to the man. Rina was not deterred. She knocked on the countertop, until the girl turned her attention back to her.

"I'm Rina Roberts, and I believe you paged me?"

Both the young girl and the sequoia-size man turned to stare at her. The man's all too intense gaze made Rina incredibly nervous, not to mention a few degrees warmer. She wasn't accustomed to being the sole object of a man's attention. Especially one who looked like him.

"Ms. Roberts?" The man's voice, deep, intense and incredibly calm caused her to turn and look at him, something she'd avoided doing since she'd stepped to the counter. "Rina Roberts?" he asked with a lift of his brow.

"Yes," she said cautiously, turning to him. Her heart immediately skipped into a staccato rhythm, surprising her.

"I'm Dr. Blackwell. Dr. Hunter Blackwell. Billy's godfather."

Chapter Two

Rina's mouth fell open like a trapdoor that had suddenly sprung open and she tipped her head back to take him in—all of him.

Instinctively, her hand fluttered to her heart. It had almost stopped when she realized who he was.

From the way James had always talked about the kindly Dr. Blackwell, she'd been expecting someone like…Dr. Spock. Old, comfortable Dr. Spock.

Now *that* was a pediatrician, not this…this…man who looked like an ancient warrior from the past.

He was tall, towering over her five-foot-two frame, and he wore well-worn jeans that lovingly caressed his strong, muscled legs. His equally well-worn chambray shirt, left open at the collar and rolled up at the sleeves, covered shoulders that looked like they'd have trouble fitting through a barn door. An open barn door.

His sleek black hair, a black unlike anything she'd ever seen except for on her sister-in-law, Jane, was long and pulled back off his face in a ponytail, probably for comfort as well as appearance.

His skin was a beautiful shade of bronze, a testament to his Native American ancestry no doubt. But that face...mother of mercy. That face was harsh and weathered from the sun, yet achingly beautiful in a blatantly masculine way. All sharp planes and angles, he had high cheekbones, full lips, and eyes that were so dark, so wide she wondered if they were capable of seeing past whatever facade people presented to him.

"Would you like to see my teeth?" Hunter inquired, amused, and trying not to smile at the look of embarrassment that flooded her eyes, and flushed her cheeks. He'd long ago accepted the peculiarities of others. They had no idea that in his culture staring was considered highly offensive, a personal insult at best.

Furious at herself for her behavior, Rina swallowed hard. "Ex...cuse me?"

She was absolutely certain the heat had fried her brains, and stolen her manners. Never in her life had she ever so blatantly stared at a man before. But then again, she thought miserably, she'd never quite been this startled by a man before.

"My teeth," Hunter said patiently. "Since you've

uh…obviously inspected everything else…would you uh…like to see…anything else?''

The flush started at her neck, and swiftly moved upward until her cheeks were stained as if someone had dotted them with cherry juice.

Hunter couldn't remember the last time he'd seen a woman blush. In spite of his own feelings, he found it incredibly charming.

''No, no, no.'' Rina shook her head, mortified beyond belief. ''I'm sorry,'' she said hurriedly, averting her gaze, trying to look everywhere but at him, remembering too late that in his culture staring was considered the height of rudeness and disrespect. ''It's…it's just…I was expecting…Dr. Spock.''

''Dr. Spock?'' Hunter repeated with a slight lift of his brow, trying to understand. He shook his head as recognition dawned. ''Ms. Roberts,'' he said with an easy smile. ''This is Texas, not the starship *Enterprise*.''

''No, not *Mr.* Spock,'' she corrected, trying to stop blushing. She was clearly not making a very good impression. ''*Dr.* Spock,'' she clarified, trying to explain, and failing miserably, judging from the amusement shimmering from those dark eyes. ''You know…the pediatrician,'' she concluded lamely, only amusing him more. ''From the way James always described you I thought…well…I just thought…'' Her voice trailed off when she realized she was just making the situation worse.

''I see.'' In an effortless move, he took her overnight case from her, transferring it from her hand to his. "So does this mean you expect all pediatricians to be old, wrinkled and have white hair?"

Fanning her face, she managed a smile, grateful he at least had a sense of humor.

"I'm sorry, I'm exhausted and a bit punchy from lack of sleep." She shrugged. "I assure you I'm usually a bit more articulate, not to mention a bit more polite. I guess you just weren't what I expected."

Taking her elbow, he nodded, guiding her toward the double electronic doors that would take them outdoors.

Anxious to stop embarrassing herself, she followed him toward the doors, glancing around, lifting her chin to look into his eyes.

She felt as if the ground had shifted beneath her. Mother of mercy, those eyes of his were like fathomless pools, and looking into them made her blood heat and slow.

Hunter glanced down at her just as she glanced up. He felt it, too, that inexplicable click of recognition, of something so ethereal it had no name. He only knew that for the first time in a long, long time, he realized he'd have to be cautious around a woman. Very cautious.

He'd worked too hard for his inner peace to have it disrupted by a beautiful woman. Especially a beautiful woman who had no need or knowledge of his life, his culture, or his ways. More importantly, no need of him. He'd do well to remember that.

Struggling to rein in her thoughts, Rina swallowed hard and averted her gaze, looking around him.

"How's Billy? Or rather, where's Billy?" she immediately clarified, letting her worry get the best of her as she continued to look around him for some sign of her nephew.

"Billy's with his grandfather," he said carefully, looking down at her with some concern as they headed toward the doors. As a doctor, he didn't like her coloring. "And he's fine."

The double doors swished open with a hiss, and he guided her out into the late-afternoon sunshine.

The heat hit Rina again, making her catch her breath. Closing her eyes, she didn't realize her legs wobbled, until he caught her elbow with one hand.

She felt his touch like a sucker punch, and caught her breath. His fingers were long, slim and smooth, his palm soft, and incredibly gentle.

His brows drew together a bit as he continued to look at her. "It's you I'm worried about at the moment." Her eyes were wide, her cheeks flushed, not from embarrassment this time, but from the heat.

Rina's legs seemed to lose more strength, and she struggled to hold herself upright. The way his eyes were going over her face made her feel as if he'd just touched her, caressed her, the way a lover would caress a cherished woman he was about to make love to.

It made her breath quicken, which only added to her sudden light-headedness. Her eyes slid closed and she teetered a bit.

"When was the last time you had anything to eat?" His voice had taken on the harshness of concern. She'd lost all color and her eyes were wide and glassy.

Rina swallowed, praying her legs weren't going to buckle. "Eat?" she repeatedly weakly. "You mean like food?"

Just the thought made her stomach flip and she moaned slightly, pressing her free hand to her roiling tummy. She was a bad flyer at best. Couple that with her distress over her brother's death, and the situation with Billy, and she hadn't been able to choke down a bite in days.

"Yeah, food." Frowning, he tightened his hold on her elbow. "Life's nourishment."

"I...I...don't remember," she admitted honestly, then had to swallow again when she realized he was looking at her in a way that made her pulse skid.

"Well, the first thing we need to do is get you out of those clothes—"

Addled or not, she came to an abrupt halt, turning to stare up at him with such an arch look he laughed.

"I guess that didn't come out quite right." He laughed again, and his dark eyes glinted with what she assumed was amusement and one dark brow lifted. "Don't be alarmed. I'm a doctor, remember?"

"I remember," she corrected with a decided frown. The thought of this man getting her out of her clothes caused an immediate image to spring into her mind.

Him.

And her.

Without any clothes.

Doctor or no doctor, where on earth had that thought come from?

Scrambling to banish the image, Rina tried to focus on her words, and not her errant, absolutely ridiculous thoughts.

Rina pressed a hand to her forehead. Mother of mercy what on earth was wrong with her?

She wasn't the kind of woman who had X-rated thoughts in the middle of the afternoon, especially about a man she'd just met and barely knew.

It was the heat. Absolutely. It was scrambling her brains, and wreaking havoc on her common sense.

"Yes, I remember you're a doctor," she said, pushing the hair off her face and struggling for some dignity. A few, steady steps wouldn't be bad either. "But when I meet a man and the first thing he says is 'let's get you out of those clothes,' it has a tendency to make a woman...worry, especially a practical Midwestern woman," she added with a decided frown.

And especially *this* woman, she wanted to add, but didn't. Men didn't go around trying to get her out of her clothes. Men simply never thought of her that way. It was a fact of life she'd known and grown to understand a long time ago.

Perhaps that's why she was so stunned.

Hunter tightened his fingers on her arm as he led

her toward the parking lot. She was vividly aware of the heat of his skin, the touch of his hand.

"I imagine a lot of men have said the same thing," he countered easily, "but my intentions were purely honorable and medicinal," he clarified, but his words did little to comfort her. "By the time we get to the ranch, Sadie will just about have dinner ready." He smiled, holding on to her arm tightly—just in case she decided to take a nosedive. "Some lighter weight clothing, a cool shower, a decent meal and a good night's sleep and hopefully, you'll feel much, much better."

"No, wait." Alarmed, Rina came to a stop, placing a hand on her spinning head. "I can't stay at your house, and I certainly can't impose on your wife." It was ridiculous to feel such a stab of disappointment, she realized. She should have realized he would be married.

"Yes, you *can* stay at my house," he insisted, "since it's either that or sleep under the stars." That widened her eyes, making him smile. He wished she didn't look so fragile, so pale. "There isn't a hotel or motel anywhere near the reservation. We're in the boonies, remember?" He took her arm and started walking again, anxious to get her out of the heat. "And Sadie's not my wife, she's the Blackwell family housekeeper and the best cook in all of Texas." His gaze shifted to her mouth and Rina felt her stomach somersault. "I'm not married," he added softly.

The look in his eyes was as hot as a caress, but she couldn't seem to stop staring at him.

"Why?" she blurted before she could stop herself.

One brow rose in interest. "Why is Sadie the Blackwell family housekeeper?" he asked carefully, still looking at her in amusement. "Or why aren't I married?"

"B-both," she stammered, still unnerved by the way he was looking at her.

Instinctively, he gave in to the need to touch her, and gently ran a fingertip down her cheek, wiping a smudge of travel dust from her. Her skin was warm and smooth, like the finest silk.

Rina's eyes widened and she swallowed, trying to maintain some dignity.

Hunter continued to look at her, as if drawn by some invisible force. The emotions swirling around inside him, the sudden tightening in his loins, the inexplicable need to touch, to hold, probably should have alarmed him.

He'd been down this road before; he'd already had a woman cloud his mind, and tangle his emotions, but at the moment, he was too concerned with *her* physical well-being to worry about whether or not he should be worried about *his* own emotional well-being.

He laughed suddenly, breaking the tension. "Sadie's been with my folks since right after they married. My parents retired to Florida about a year ago after my dad's heart attack, and Sadie stayed here to 'take care of her boys.'"

"Her boys?" Rina asked with a frown.

"Me and my brothers," he clarified as he continued to lead her toward his truck. "Of course the fact that we're all grown and in or nearing our thirties doesn't matter one whit to Sadie. She still treats us like we were five, and incorrigible at best." He slanted a glance at her, pleased to see some of her color returning. "And I'm not married because I believe a man can only have one love in his life at a time, and mine's my practice at the moment. It takes all my time and attention." It wasn't exactly a lie, he reasoned. "I'm on staff at the hospital in town, as well as run the tribal clinic, and it doesn't leave much time for a social life."

Until this moment, it suited him fine. Now, he realized he'd been neglecting some of life's basic pleasures.

But that didn't give him a reason to forget the lessons of his past.

At least not with this woman.

"I see," Rina said, relieved and ridiculously pleased that he wasn't married, and not quite certain why.

"Here we are." Hunter hustled her to a stop in front of his truck, then tossed her bags in the back before opening the door for her.

"Get in," he said with a nod, giving her a gentle nudge to get her moving.

With a weary sigh, Rina climbed into the large red pickup. Although it was covered with dust, it was new, and in excellent condition.

Climbing behind the wheel, Hunter pulled his

sunglasses from his shirt pocket and slipped them back on before starting the ignition.

"Hunter, please don't get me wrong. I appreciate your offer of hospitality, I really do, but I think the first order of business is to see Billy." Shifting her legs, she settled herself more comfortably in the seat, grateful for the blast of cool, fresh air from the air-conditioning. Leaning her head back, she sighed, letting her eyes slide closed for a moment. "Right now, it's all I can think about—the only thing I've been able to think about since this all happened."

"I understand," he said softly, laying a gentle hand over hers. It was clear she cared deeply for the boy, but that, unfortunately, did not change things. It would take more than love and caring for this woman to be able to raise an Apache child in her world.

It would take nothing less than a miracle since there was no way this woman would ever be able to have custody of Billy. Not with tribal laws the way they were.

Billy was her nephew, yes, but he was still half Apache. A half-breed child, Hunter mentally corrected, as he pulled into traffic, knowing all too well, as a half-breed himself, exactly what raising a child like that entailed.

She was clearly no more prepared for the task than his mother had been. She knew nothing of Native American ways—their life, their culture—nor did she understand what Billy meant to the tribe.

Glancing at Rina, he realized now wasn't the time

to tell her. Nor could he let his own past cloud Billy's future. But facts were facts. He would need some time, time to break this news to her, to make her understand that what she wanted—Billy—was impossible.

And never going to happen.

Rina sighed, letting her eyes close, and relaxing a bit now that she was out of the direct heat.

"I just can't stop thinking about Billy," she admitted, extracting a tissue from her handbag and wiping her nose.

"I understand."

"I wasn't much older than Billy when my own parents were killed and I know how devastating it can be." Opening her eyes, she turned her head to look at him. "At least I had James," she said, smiling sadly in remembrance. "It was both a blessing and a curse."

One brow rose and Hunter shifted his gaze from the road to look at her. "What do you mean?"

"It was a blessing because at least I wasn't totally alone, and it was also a curse because the responsibility of raising James was mine alone." She sighed wistfully. "At times I wished I would have had the benefit of an adult to guide me. It was like flying blind without a parachute." She looked at him. "At least now, with Billy, I've had some experience."

"You apparently did a wonderful job," he said, hoping to get off the subject of her raising Billy, at least for now. "Your brother was a fine man and a good husband and father."

She nodded. It was the first time he'd mentioned James, and then she remembered. In his culture it was considered disrespectful to speak of the dead.

She was going to have to pay particular attention to the little bit of knowledge James had shared with her about the Native American culture—if she didn't want to go around insulting the man.

Another task, Rina thought with a sigh, pushing her hair off her face. "Thank you. I know he was very happy here. When he first said he was going to marry Jane Eaglefeather, and live on the reservation, I was stunned." She smiled to soften her words. At his look, she rushed on. "Not because she was Native American," she explained, "but simply because having James choose another life for himself, one that albeit made him happy, but one that meant he'd move thousands of miles away seemed as if I was losing a part of my family all over again." She smiled, smoothing down her skirt. "But once I realized how happy he was, and he *was* happy," she said firmly, "I knew it was for the best. I guess that's why it was so important for me to come here to Texas right away. I wanted to let Billy know he's not alone. That he still has family. That he still has me, and that I love and want him." She swallowed past the lump in her throat.

"I understand, Rina." And he did, but still, that didn't change things. She could never have or take the boy from the reservation. "I'm sure Billy knows how you feel about him,'' he said with an easy smile, hoping to soften the blow of his next words. ''And I know how anxious you must be to see him, but the Shaman has taken Billy to his summer hogan so that he can tell Billy about his parents and help the boy come to terms with his parents' deaths.''

Her head lifted and she merely stared at him, stunned, and more than a little annoyed.

''You mean Billy's not even here?'' She shook her head with a frown. ''But his grandfather knew I was coming. Why on earth would he take Billy to his summer hogan?'' She shook her head again. ''I don't understand.''

Carefully, he measured his words. ''Death, at least death in our culture is not the same as in yours, and you must remember, Billy has been raised on the reservation. His whole life has been lived learning the Holy-Life Way of The People. *His* people,'' he added softly. ''He's going to have to come to terms with this in his own way, the way he's been raised.''

''I can understand that,'' she said carefully. What she didn't understand was why Billy couldn't understand the situation *here*. Why it had been necessary for his grandfather to take him somewhere where she couldn't see him. Immediately.

''We believe life is merely a cycle,'' Hunter continued, ''and when the Death Spirit calls, we simply leave this world to become one with the universe, like all living things—plants, animals, etc.'' He shrugged his massive shoulders. ''Our bodies are considered merely an outer shell. It is our souls that are important. Death is just a perfectly natural cycle for all living things.''

''So you're saying that this will seem natural to Billy? Just another part of life?'' she asked with a frown, trying to understand.

''Yes. Right now, in order for Billy to find some peace with what's happened, it's important for him to remember the life lessons he's been taught. Going to his grandfather's summer hogan, where he can fish and hunt, and be one with the nature will help him find his Peace with his parents' passing.''

He made it seem so natural, so dispassionate. ''Is that why Billy didn't want to come to Chicago for his father's funeral?''

It had hurt, but she'd tried to understand that James had chosen a different path for his life, and his family. A path she might not fully have understood, but nevertheless had accepted and respected.

''Yes.'' He paused to make a left turn that would take them toward his ranch. ''The Apache don't believe in the traditional Christian values of death and dying, heaven or hell. God is not a deity we understand. We believe in a Creator, *Yusin*—The Life Giver, but he is benevolent, not punitive, nor do we worship him in the Christian manner. Billy has no knowledge or understanding of the Christian ritual of burial. He believes as we all do that his parents' souls have now become one with the universe. To have him attend such a ceremony would only frighten and confuse him. This way, by going with his grandfather, by hunting and fishing and being one with nature, Billy will feel as if he's still with his parents, and that he's honoring them in a manner he's been taught.''

She was struggling to let her annoyance go so she could understand. ''So then what you're saying is that Billy will not look at this as a tragedy, but merely as just another cycle of life.''

''Yes, but don't make the mistake of thinking that he will not grieve. He's suffered a tremendous loss, and loss is the same in any culture. But right now, it's important for Billy to come to terms with his parents' deaths in the only way he knows.'' He glanced at her. ''Do you understand?''

She frowned, trying not to be alarmed or angry by the fact that she wasn't going to see her nephew right away after all.

''I guess I do, but I have to be honest with you. I know the Shaman has been ill, and I'm concerned about his health and whether or not Billy will be...'' Embarrassed, her voice trailed off, and Hunter glanced at her.

''Safe?'' he finished for her, looking at her carefully. He felt that inexplicable pull when he looked at her, trying to concentrate on her words, not on his own feelings. ''You're worried about Billy being safe with his grandfather?''

He would not be offended, he told himself. It was a natural reaction from someone who had no understanding of the Holy-Life Ways.

Carefully, he chose his words. ''I can understand

your concerns, Rina, but you must understand, in our culture, age is a virtue. We respect our elders for their wisdom, their knowledge, and the blessings they've given to their people. Although it's true that the Shaman has been ill, you must remember, Billy is the most important thing in his grandfather's life. He would never do anything to jeopardize the boy's safety. And they're not alone,'' he added. ''Hallie Lost Souls is with them.''

''Hallie Lost Souls?'' Her brows drew together, wondering if he thought she'd find that comforting. ''I hope his name isn't indicative of anything.''

Hunter laughed as he flipped on his direction signal to turn into the long winding driveway of his ranch.

''Hallie has been the Shaman's best friend for as long as I can remember. His devotion to the Shaman is legendary. It is said many years ago that the Shaman did a great favor for Hallie, one he never forgot. Since that time, you rarely see the Shaman without Hallie. Especially now that the Shaman's health is poor. Hallie looks out for him, and cares for him.'' He patted her hand as he came to a stop. ''Billy is fine, I assure you.'' His gaze went over her again, and his eyebrows drew together. ''And perhaps it's better if you get some food and rest before you see Billy. It would only upset him more to see you in this condition.'' Unable to resist touching her, he gently laid a hand on her cheek. It was cool now and as soft as a baby. Something about this woman was drawing him. It was disconcerting. "Please don't worry. I promise you Billy is safe."

Annoyed now, in spite of his assurances, but too addled by his touch to be able to think clearly, she nodded.

"I'll try not to worry," she answered finally, once he removed his hand. Her fingers, her hand was still tingling from his touch. Absently, she rubbed it across the material of her skirt. "But I have to tell you, worrying is part of my nature." She frowned as he threw open the door to hop out. "It's probably what I do best. Hunter?" she called, scrambling after him out of the truck. "Exactly when will Billy and the Shaman return?"

Hunter shrugged, then smiled, hoping to allay some of the concern he saw shimmering in her dark eyes. "Soon," he said evasively, making her frown again.

"Soon," she repeated, dubious in spite of his explanation. Rina tried not to let her worry get the best of her. But she suddenly had an uneasy feeling.

A very uneasy feeling.

The Shaman knew she was coming to speak to him about Billy's care and welfare, as well as his custody.

Why would he leave before seeing her? Before discussing something that was so important?

In spite of Hunter's explanation, it simply didn't make sense. It was as if the Shaman didn't want her to see her nephew.

The thought brought on almost an irrational sense of panic.

She glanced at Hunter again as he began to unload her gear, and wondered why she had an uncanny feeling he wasn't telling her the truth.

At least not the whole truth.

Chapter Three

Nervous in spite of Hunter's assurances that she wasn't imposing, and also feeling uneasy simply because of the circumstances, Rina reluctantly followed Hunter as he made his way up the long, winding driveway of the sprawling ranch house, wishing she were somewhere—anywhere—else, doing anything else.

But she had to be here, she realized with a sigh. Had to stay until the Shaman brought her nephew back from the canyon.

She could only hope her idea of *soon* and Hunter's bore some resemblance.

She heard the bark of a dog as well as the raised voices of what appeared to be several men.

"I'm telling you that ball was foul."

"Foul! It was clearly in. Every time you miss a basket you claim foul."

"If you'd put your glasses on, you'd be able to see that ball was foul."

Rounding the house, Hunter came to a stop with a shake of his head, watching as a large Irish setter barked and jumped and wound his way between the legs of his two brothers who were standing toe-to-toe glaring at one another. Only the basketball perched between their stomachs kept them at bay.

"Are you two at it again?" Hunter asked with an indulgent smile and another shake of his head. He turned to Rina. "Meet my brothers. Cutter and Colt."

Rina stared at all three men. She turned to Hunter, one brow raised. "Your brothers?"

Amused, and quite used to the reaction, he nodded. "Absolutely."

"I see," she said, not seeing anything of the kind. While Hunter was obviously Native American, the other two men, although as big as Hunter, with hair just as black, were decidedly *not*.

"We were all adopted by the Blackwells," he said by way of explanation, setting down her overnight case just as one of his brothers tossed the basketball at him. He caught it just before it connected with his nose.

"Cutter! Colt!" Hunter called, interrupting the heated basketball discussion.

Both men turned toward him, and their faces instantly relaxed into smiles as they took Rina in.

"This is Rina Roberts. Billy's aunt. And our guest," he added with a great deal more emphasis than necessary. "Show you've got some manners.

"Ahhh, an unbiased judge." One of Hunter's brothers—she didn't know which one yet—took her by the hand. "Obviously you're a wise, intelligent knowledgeable woman. Come on, you can be the judge." He glanced down at her. "I'm Colt by the way." He grinned a rakish grin, then reached for her hand. "The best looking of the brothers."

In spite of her own unease, Rina found herself chuckling at the man's obvious charm. She glanced at all three men again.

She'd be hard-pressed to choose the best looking of the bunch. All three were incredibly gorgeous in their own distinctive way.

Colt was a few inches shorter than Hunter, with a shock of thick black curly hair that fell rakishly over his forehead and wide, expressive blue eyes that were as clear and bright as a sapphire. He definitely had the look of the devil in those eyes, she thought with a smile. She had a feeling this one had been a handful as a boy, and was probably more so now as an adult.

He wore ragged cutoffs that exposed deeply tanned legs, and a sleeveless sweatshirt that had more holes than material.

Although he didn't physically resemble Hunter, except for the shock of black hair, they shared the same charming smile.

"Stop trying to influence the judge," Cutter com-

plained good-naturedly, taking Rina's other hand
and trying to tug her loose from Colt, who stead-
fastly held on.

Cutter was just a shade taller than both of his
brothers, but still had the same black hair, although
his was just a bit shaggy, and worn long enough to
curl at his neck. Like Hunter, Cutter's eyes were a
deep, dark brown, but she couldn't say they were
friendly, more wary. Very wary. It surprised her. His
gaze swept over her in one glance, as if assessing
and categorizing, before coming to some conclusion.

"I...I...don't know much about basketball," she
stammered, trying to free herself as she glanced
back at Hunter in alarm.

"That's okay," Colt said, still grinning. "You've
got eyes, and if you can count, you're in." He
pointed. "See that row of roses over there?"

"Roses?" Rina looked where he pointed. She
nodded. "Yes, I see them."

"That's the foul line. If the ball bounces past
there it's a foul." He turned to glare at Cutter. "We
need a judge who can at least *see*."

"No," Hunter countered, garnering a glare from
both his brothers, "that's not the foul line. Those
are Mom's prized roses and if Sadie gets wind of
you guys trampling through them again, she's gonna
have all our hides."

With Cutter and Colt still holding on to her hands,
the big Irish setter decided to get into the act. He
gave a great loud woof, then pounced, jumping up
and planting his large paws heavily on Rina's chest,

knocking the breath from her. She gave a squeal as she lost her balance and fell backward.

"Baby, down!" Hunter scolded, swatting the dog with one hand, and catching Rina with the other.

Before she knew what had happened, Cutter had released her hand and caught the large dog by the scruff of his collar to hold him at bay, whispering softly to him to calm him down. He moved so fast she hadn't even seen it.

With Hunter's arms warm and secure around her, and her back pressed against his wide chest, Rina felt her knees go wobbly again.

There was power and strength in his arms, his body, and for a moment, she allowed herself the pleasure of leaning against him.

It was a luxury she'd rarely had in her life. She'd been alone and done so many things alone that having someone to lean on, if only for a moment, seemed like a rare and precious gift.

She could feel the pounding of his heart, smell the distinctly masculine scent of him and suddenly felt intoxicated by his scent, his presence.

Rattled more than she believed possible, Rina let her eyes slide closed to savor the sudden feelings— foreign feelings—that gripped her, wishing her heart would slow and her legs would steady.

Encircled in his arms, for the first time in memory she felt...safe. It was a feeling she couldn't ever remember feeling. It frightened her.

"Hey," Hunter whispered softly, tightening his arms around her, stunned by the sudden impact of having that sweet, feminine body pressed against his. "Are you all right?"

Holding her in his arms, Hunter shifted her so that he could see her face. His own heart felt like a jackhammer and he could swear his palms were sweating just from her nearness.

Rina's eyes opened and her breath caught at his closeness.

Only an inch or so away, she could see her own reflection in his eyes, feel his warm breath fan her cheek. It made her legs grow wobbly again, and she was grateful she was leaning against him, certain she would have fallen otherwise.

Hunter watched her, stunned by his body's instinctive reaction to her. It seemed a betrayal on the most intimate, basic level. Emotionally and intellectually he knew better than to allow himself these kinds of feelings for this woman.

Any woman.

Hadn't he learned his lesson?

First from his mother? Then Meagan?

Did he have to get hit over the head once again for the information to sink in?

Women were not to be trusted. On any level. For any reason.

He'd do well to remember that.

He was trying, desperately, but it was hard with Rina's sweet delicate curves pressing against him, and the exotic scent of her perfume infiltrating his breathing space.

She was as delicate and fragile as he'd thought.

He shifted her again, so that she wouldn't know of his sudden desire for her, desire that had started the moment he'd laid eyes on her, and only increased in intensity since then.

Her mouth was so close, if he bent his head a fraction, he could taste her, sample her, savor her. It was suddenly a deep yearning inside him, to know her taste, to feel her softness.

It rattled him as nothing had in a long while. He could not allow himself to become emotionally involved or attached to this woman. It could be disastrous for all involved. He struggled to keep his voice level, not quite ready to release her yet.

"Baby's an oaf, but she wouldn't hurt anyone." He smiled that beautiful smile that made it seem as if someone had turned up the sun a notch. "She was just playing."

"What the devil are you boys doing now? And who let that mongrel loose?"

The sound of the stern, female voice had Rina scrambling to stand on her own two feet, embarrassed at being caught in Hunter's embrace.

A stout, sturdy woman with pewter hair pulled tight into a bun, and a face as round and full as a cue ball huffed around the house, brandishing a wooden spoon.

She wore a floral print housedress, a crisp white apron, and an oversize pair of red reading glasses that made her eyes look as wide as an owl's.

"And if I find out you boys have been trampling my roses again, I'll take a switch to you. Both of you," she said, waving her spoon at Cutter and Colt. "Grown or not."

"Uh-oh," Cutter muttered, still holding the dog, who was barking and straining to get free. Cutter glanced at his brother. "Now you've done it," he accused. "Sadie's mad at us." Cutter sighed, trying to bank a smile. "Again."

"Me?" Colt drew back, offended. "I'm not the one who's so blind he can't see the foul line."

"And who's that you've got there, Hunter?" Sadie moved closer, looking as if she'd mow down anything in her path.

She peered over her reading glasses at Rina, gave her a thorough going over from head to toe, then allowed her face to soften in a welcome smile. "Why lookee here. Aren't you a pretty little thing?"

Embarrassed, Rina glanced at Hunter who merely shrugged and smiled.

Sadie stepped closer to her. "You must be Billy's Aunt Rina. We've been expecting you." Sadie held out her hand, wiping it first down the front of the apron knotted at her waist. "I'm Sadie, and I take care of this motley crew." She pumped Rina's hand like an old spigot, still appraising her. "We were real sorry to hear about your brother, honey. He was a good man. Yes indeed, a real good man." She released Rina's hand and narrowed her gaze and glared at Hunter. "And didn't your momma teach you better than to keep a guest out here baking in the heat?"

"Yes, ma'am," Hunter said. He was still standing

close enough to Rina to feel her body heat. It was hard to concentrate on his thoughts, and not on his suddenly aching body.

She shook her head. "These boys don't have the sense of a jackass," Sadie complained, looking at Rina again. "And don't you two be laughing," Sadie scolded, rounding on Cutter and Colt and shaking her wooden spoon at them.

"She's like Baby," Hunter whispered in Rina's ear, sending chills down her spine as his breath fanned the sensitive skin on her neck. It took all his restraint not to slide his lips across the silky smoothness of her neck just to see what she tasted like. "All bark and no bite."

Sadie muscled between Cutter and Colt, glaring up at them. "And you two ain't much better." She shook her head. "Old as you are playing games in the yard, tearing up the lawn and ruining my roses." She narrowed her gaze on them. "I've got a good mind to call your mama in Florida and tell her what's what."

"Come on Sadie," Colt cajoled, dropping an arm around her ample shoulders and giving her an affectionate hug. "You're not gonna tattle on us, are you?" He winked at Rina, not bothering to smother a smile. "Now, you know we didn't mean any harm." Colt planted a kiss on Sadie's chubby cheek and she blushed clear to the tips of her silver hair. "We were just having fun." He bussed her again, making a great smacking noise. "Wanna come out and play with us?'' he teased, wiggling his brows at her.

''You go on now,'' she said, still blushing as she pressed an affectionate hand to his chest. ''Did enough ball playing with you boys when you were young'uns.'' She nodded her head as she spoke. ''Ran me ragged you did. Especially you, Colt. Always into mischief.'' She gave him a gentle poke with her elbow, but there was a smile lurking around her mouth, and love in her eyes.

Straightening, she smoothed her hair back and pressed a hand to her apron. ''Ain't got time to be playing games with you three hooligans. Got dinner to fix and a table to set. Someone's gotta handle things around here now that your mama and daddy have gone south.''

She turned to Rina. ''Come on now, honey, don't you pay no mind to these renegade boys. They'd let you wilt here in this heat if I let them.'' She took Rina's hand and started moving toward the house with Rina securely in tow. ''Let's get you out of this heat. And a cool drink wouldn't hurt none, either.'' Sadie turned back for a moment to issue one final order to the three brothers.

''Now Hunter, you go on up and set Rina's gear in the guest bedroom in the west wing.'' She shifted her gaze to Cutter and Colt. ''And you two get that mongrel back in the shed where he belongs, then get washed up for dinner. You hear?''

All three brothers nodded solemnly, then exchanged amused glances.

"And Colt, you put something decent on. You're not coming to my Sunday dinner table dressed like a hooligan. No siree." She narrowed her gaze on the three of them again. "Any questions?"

All three brothers exchanged amused glances. "No ma'am," they said in unison.

"Didn't think so." Satisfied, Sadie nodded, then marched away with Rina in tow.

Dinner passed quickly. It was a loud, raucous affair during which the Blackwell brothers bantered and bickered, laughed and ate.

Rina had watched silently, amazed and a little in awe. Not having a family had deprived her of the friendly camaraderie and companionship that flowed and ebbed during something so simple as a family dinner.

She tried to bite back the stab of envy she felt, while wondering if the Blackwells knew how lucky they were.

It was what she'd always wished for herself. And for Billy. But she knew it was impossible.

But she'd make it possible, at least for Billy, she thought fiercely. She'd be the family that she'd never had; give Billy all the things she and James had missed. Love. Security. Stability. And more importantly: a family.

She'd be Billy's family, she thought with determination. All and everything he'd ever need. With love, she truly believed anything was possible.

No, it wouldn't make up for the devastating loss

Billy had suffered. She knew firsthand that nothing could do that. But perhaps, just knowing that she was there for him—now and forever—with unconditional, unending love might ease the pain of the loss a bit.

Sitting between Colt and Cutter, and across from Hunter, Rina had taken it all in, amazed at how comfortable she felt, considering the circumstances.

In just a few hours, everyone had gone out of their way to make her feel at home. In spite of her worry and concerns about Billy, and her uneasy attraction to Hunter, she found that she'd finally begun to relax.

After Sadie had hustled her inside, she'd led her to a spacious guest room with its own private bath, unpacked her clothing, then left her alone to take a shower and change in preparation for dinner.

Fortunately, Rina had thought ahead and brought some shorts and T-shirts, anticipating the intense Texas heat.

After a long, cool shower, a couple of aspirins, and a tall, refreshing glass of lemonade—left on the nightstand, courtesy of Sadie—she felt like a new woman.

"You're not eating." Hunter's deep voice stirred Rina out of her thoughts, and she glanced up guiltily, realizing almost everyone had finished eating and left the table.

Except her and Hunter.

She glanced around, uncomfortable because Hunter's dark, fathomless eyes were on her again, studying, assessing, and making her incredibly nervous and vividly aware of him.

With a sigh, she pushed her still-full plate away. "I guess I'm not really hungry." How did he expect her to eat when those gorgeous eyes were constantly on her?

Hunter kept watching her, annoyed and aware of the warming of his blood. It had been slowly heating since she'd come down to dinner in a pair of short, sexy white shorts and a T-shirt that gently caressed the outline of her small breasts under the thin cotton. Her hair, that beautiful riot of vibrant red, was still damp from her shower, and she'd pulled it back up into a topknot, but several errant strands had sprung loose to sexily frame her face and caress her slender neck.

She was barefoot, and the sight of the long expanse of her legs nearly had his tongue lolling out of his mouth.

In spite of the fact that Rina looked even more fragile and vulnerable, the sight of her sexy outfit had set his blood to simmering.

He'd been watching her carefully during dinner. Dressed as she was, she looked smaller somehow, but just as vulnerable. It was wreaking havoc with his intentions to think of her as an adversary.

His gaze slowly went over her again. He wasn't the least bit amazed to learn that hidden under all that material of her suit, she had a glorious body. All feminine curves and delicate roundness; it was enough to make a man drool.

His fingers itched to trace the line of her jaw, to run the slender length of her arm, to feel the soft plumpness of her breasts in his hands, his mouth, to feel the bareness of her legs tangled with his.

It had been a long, long time since he'd felt such an instant stir of emotions about a woman. It wasn't just a testosterone test, but something much more. Something that touched him not just physically, but emotionally as well.

It scared the hell out of him, making him wonder what the hell had gotten into him. Had he forgotten what women had the power to do to him?

He knew better than to allow his emotions to get tangled up over a woman. Especially *this* woman with the complicated situation between them.

Once burned, twice shy they always said.

Or in his case twice burned. *Always* shy.

He'd deliberately shied away from any encounters or entanglements with the opposite sex, knowing his judgment about women was somewhere on the other side of ludicrous.

Not until he laid eyes on Rina Roberts did his resolve, and his fortitude, desert him.

In spite of the warning whispering in his brain, he couldn't help himself. He reached across the table and laid a hand over hers, giving in to the need to touch her.

''Rina?'' Her skin was as silky as satin and just as warm; her fingers were long, slender and incredibly sexy.

He had an urge to lift her hand and kiss the tip

of each and every slender finger. And then slowly work his way over the rest of her, nibbling, tasting, licking, savoring.

Disconcerted by his touch, she raised her eyes to his. "Y-yes?"

Their gazes met, held, clung. He felt that inexplicable sense of…yearning. That was the only way to describe it. It was unlike anything he'd ever felt before with a woman. Not even Meagan, whom he'd been certain he'd been in love with, had stirred this kind of reaction in him.

The impact of his reaction to Rina had Hunter's blood thudding in his ears, and in far more sensitive parts of his body, reminding him that he was treading on very dangerous ground, with a very dangerous woman.

A woman who looked more like a timid librarian, than a sultry temptress.

But then again, he'd learned a long time ago that looks could be deceiving.

Especially when it came to women.

He was older, wiser. Emotionally he knew better than to get involved with another woman who had no understanding of him, his life or his ways.

But when he looked at Rina, and felt that gut-wrenching yearning that was not subject to reason, or intellect, it was not as easy to remember the searing pain or the gut-burning anger of the past.

Wanting to ease some of the discomfort hardening his body and thickening his blood, he shifted his gaze to her mouth and instantly regretted it.

Rina's soft, unpainted mouth was lush, full and looked as delectable as the apple in Eden.

When her tongue flicked out to gently dampen her lower lip, his fists clenched in frustration as he watched the slow, sensuous motion of her tongue.

Stunned speechless, Rina continued to stare at him, wondering what was happening to her; what he was doing to her.

His eyes seemed to have darkened, if that was possible, and the sight made her wonder what he was thinking.

She tried to take a breath, to get some air in her frantic lungs, but found someone seemed to have stolen all the air.

Deliberately, Hunter shifted his gaze from her mouth, then shifted his body to bring some relief, trying to banish his thoughts and bring his mind back to the present. She was staring at him the way a chicken might stare at a wolf.

She was in over her head, and it clearly showed. Obviously she had no idea what was vibrating between them, although the intensity was enough to peel the paint off the walls.

But judging from the confused look on her face, in her eyes, she didn't have a clue, which led him to believe she probably didn't have much experience with men.

It surprised him, and relieved him, but he didn't take the time to wonder why.

"You look beat," he said with a sympathetic

smile, letting his thumb stroke the softness of her hand.

Rina swallowed hard. That smile ought to be outlawed, she thought in dismay. Hunter Blackwell was an impressive man to begin with, but when he let loose that killer smile, he was almost downright…lethal.

Taking a deep breath in the hope that it would slow her racing heart, Rina glanced away for a moment before bringing her gaze back to his.

"I guess I am." Perhaps if she pleaded fatigue, she could slip upstairs to her room, and away from the intense gaze and powerful presence of Hunter.

Coward, her mind uttered. She couldn't very well hide in her room for the duration simply because she was afraid of her reaction to Hunter.

She had far too many questions and concerns about Billy to give in to such female foolishness.

She'd simply ignore the reaction she was having to this man, she decided.

Unable to keep looking at her without having his thoughts run rampant, Hunter turned and glanced toward the kitchen window.

"The sun's gone down and it's probably cooled quite a bit. Why don't we go sit on the porch for a while?"

He decided it was probably best to retrieve his hand from hers, lest he do something foolish like tug her across the table and cover that luscious bow-shaped mouth with his. Regretfully, he released her hand and stood up.

"Shall we?" A little fresh air just might cool him off as well.

A little panicked at the idea of being alone with him, Rina glanced around the kitchen. "I should probably help with the dinner dishes." Standing on shaky legs, she picked up her plate, but her hands were trembling so hard she almost dropped it.

Hunter was around the table, taking the plate from her hands before she could react. He set the plate on the counter, and took her hand again.

"Sadie doesn't allow anyone to help in her kitchen." He smiled down at her, gently leading her toward the back door. "She's very territorial, and anyone intruding on her territory is likely to get shot."

The screen door slammed shut behind them, and Rina took a deep breath of the clean night air. It didn't dissipate Hunter's intensely masculine scent, which seemed to have infiltrated the very air she was breathing, nearly intoxicating her.

Inhaling deeply through her nose, she let her breath out slowly, hoping to stave off the panic that was hovering just around the edges.

She concentrated on her surroundings, and not on the man still holding her hand, standing close enough to her so that she could feel his body heat.

It had indeed cooled down. She glanced toward the large, expansive yard, and the driveway beyond. Deep, serious darkness, she thought with a hint of a shiver. The kind of dark you never found in the city swirled around them as night sounds echoed around them. She resisted the urge to huddle just a bit closer to Hunter.

"Oh, my." Her hand went to her mouth as her eyes took in the old-fashioned wooden swing. "It's...beautiful." She crossed the porch and reverently ran a hand over the chain, as well as the brightly painted wood. "I've never actually seen an old-fashioned swing like this." She glanced back at him, surprised to find him smiling at her. Her voice and eyes had taken on a dreamy quality that touched something inside him. "At least not in person."

She ran her hand over the wood again, letting her mind conjure up all the romantic fairy tales she remembered from her childhood, when she'd sit starry-eyed in front of the television watching old, romantic movies. Each one seemed to feature a wonderful old swing, and a glamorous couple who were madly in love.

Rina sighed, remembering a time when she thought love found everyone and conquered all. Now she knew differently.

"Have a seat," Hunter said softly, startling her. He was directly behind her. If she leaned back just a bit, she'd be leaning against him. She took a step away from him, causing him to laugh.

"Rina." He laid a hand on her shoulder and she could feel the heat of his touch burn through the thin material of her shirt. "I promise I won't bite," he said softly as he tugged her down beside him on the swing. The humor in his voice made her realize she was being foolish. She had absolutely nothing to be nervous about. Hunter was just being cordial to a guest. Surely he was unaware of the reaction she was having to him, and to let him know would only embarrass both of them. She had to get a grip on herself. She may not have had a great deal of experience with men, but she wasn't a rube, either.

Well, she thought, worrying her lower lip with her teeth, perhaps her limited experience with men did qualify her as a rube, but that was certainly no reason to let Hunter know.

Obviously a man like him—a man who *looked* like him—was used to women throwing themselves at him, gawking at him, making fools of themselves in front of him.

She certainly wasn't about to sink to those adolescent levels just because she found this man incredibly attractive.

She had a higher purpose here than worrying about how she was responding to this man. It would do well to remember that.

With a reluctant sigh, Rina closed her eyes, leaned back against the swing, and stretched out her long legs, giving in to the need to stretch, to relax the strain that fatigue had brought on.

Hunter's mouth nearly dropped open as he watched those long, shapely legs extend. He couldn't seem to stop staring at her.

She had the kind of legs that could wrap around a man and hold on no matter how fast or furious the ride.

The vision leaped into his mind, stunning him for a moment. He could picture it clearly. Her naked, under him, those delicate, slender fingers raking down his back, her body arching under his, those long, glorious legs wrapped tightly around him.

He almost groaned again.

"Hunter, are you all right?" She touched his arm.

Annoyed at himself, he rubbed his hand over his eyes, trying to block the image. "I'm fine," he muttered. The touch of her hand on his arm made him feel as if he'd been seared with a branding iron.

"Are you sure?" She sounded so worried, he looked at her, touched by the concern in her eyes, her voice.

He rubbed his eyes again. "I'm fine."

"You know, you're very lucky," she said softly, as Hunter set the swing in motion. "I envy you."

"Envy me?" One brow rose as he considered. Her voice was soft, sincere. "Why's that?"

She smiled, lacing her hands together in her lap before glancing at him. "Because of your family."

He laughed. "They can be a handful," he admitted with love in his voice. "But I wouldn't trade them for anything in the world. My family means everything to me."

She sighed. "I always wanted a big family. The camaraderie between all of you, the easy smiles, the gentle love and affection..." Her voice trailed off again and he realized how deep her ache for family was. He knew, and understood, realizing he'd probably have felt the same way if Justin and Emma

Blackwell hadn't opened their hearts and their home to him.

"I guess I always wanted that easy comfort that comes from family," Rina continued. "You know, that feeling of knowing you belonged somewhere to someone." She stopped, letting her words hang in the air, afraid she'd revealed too much. It had been a long-held dream, one she'd had difficulty letting go of simply because family was so very important to her.

He slid his arm across the back of the swing behind her; his fingers absently tickled the few errant strands of hair cascading down her neck, sending a shiver over her.

"That's natural," he said quietly, touched by the yearning he heard in her voice. "So if you wanted a big family, how come you never married?"

Rina shrugged. "I don't know," she said honestly. "I guess I just never found the right man." She smiled. "I was seeing someone for a while...." Her voice trailed off self-consciously.

"And?"

"And, after two years I realized it just wasn't right." She shrugged. "And now with what's happened to James and Jane, Billy is my first priority."

"I can understand that."

She'd been lonely, he realized, trying to remember what James had told him about his family. "How old were you when your folks died?"

"Seventeen. It was so sudden and unexpected. One day my parents were there, the next they were gone forever. A car accident took them both. At least they didn't suffer.'' Her voice had softened to just a whisper that tugged at his heart. He could hear the fear, the anger and the loneliness through her words and he wanted to wrap her in his arms. Just to comfort, he assured himself, knowing it was a lie. ''James was just a boy,'' she admitted. ''And just as scared and frightened as I.'' Her chin lifted with pride, and determination. ''But I didn't have time to be frightened. I had to take care of James.''

''It couldn't have been easy.'' He lowered his arm from the swing to her shoulder, giving in to the need to comfort.

''It wasn't,'' she admitted on a long, drawn out sigh, trying to forget that frightening time when she felt so alone, and as if the weight of the world was on her young shoulders. ''But we got through it, James and I.'' Pride and love lifted her voice. She laughed suddenly, turning her head to look at Hunter, caught short by his closeness. ''But I have to tell you, I don't envy your mother. Raising one boy was enough.'' She shook her head, vividly aware of how close his powerful body was, and the impact it was having on her. She was struggling to keep her mind on their conversation, and not on his nearness. ''I can't even imagine raising three.''

''We were a handful,'' he admitted with a laugh. ''It's a miracle we all lived through it considering some of the antics we pulled.'' Memories washed over him, warm, familiar and filled with love.

''James was no angel, either,'' she admitted with

a chuckle. "And considering Billy is definitely his father's son, I imagine I'm in for another wild ride. Fourteen can be a dreadful age for boys. They're difficult, at best." Rina laughed suddenly. "Actually, at that age, boys are not fit for human company with their miserable tempers, unbundled egos and their misplaced emotions. There was a time when I was hoping for a constitutional amendment that decreed that for the duration, all teenage males would follow the tradition of the penguins."

"Penguins?" Hunter frowned. "I imagine you have a point here?" he asked with a smile.

Rina laughed. "Penguins appear to believe that once their young reach adolescence they're not fit for life among adults, so they banish all the adolescents to live together, separate and away from the adults until they *are* adults." She shook her head. "After some of the antics James pulled as a teenager, I was absolutely certain it was a sound, smart idea." She pushed a strand of hair off her cheek. "And I'm well aware of some of the antics Billy has pulled the past six months or so. Although James and I didn't see each other very often, we were very close and spoke several times a week."

She knew, too, that Billy's parents' deaths were only going to complicate things for the boy, and make him more confused, and angry. Two very dangerous emotions when dealing with an adolescent in the throes of a testosterone storm, trying to find his place in the world. "But I'm sure we'll get through it, Billy and I, just as James and I did. I imagine it will just take some time. This is obviously a very difficult situation for him, but once he's settled in Chicago, and in school, I'm hoping that he'll come around.'' She turned to Hunter, aware that he had gone suddenly still.

''So you're planning on seeking custody of Billy,'' he said quietly. Too quietly. She turned to look at him, stunned by the seriousness of his voice.

''Of course, that's why I'm here.'' Feeling unnerved, she rushed on. ''I'm Billy's only relative, other than his grandfather, and his grandfather is clearly far too ill to care for a rambunctious fourteen-year-old. I'm obviously the logical choice to raise Billy, don't you agree?''

The question hung in the air for a long moment, making her incredibly nervous. An owl hooted overhead, and the moon seemed to shift, casting a shadow over the porch. And her heart.

''Hunter?'' She studied him, feeling that sense of unease again. It struck her then with such clarity she wondered why she hadn't realized it before. ''You don't think I should have custody of Billy, do you?''

Chapter Four

The squeaking of the porch swing was the only sound for long moments. Overhead, the moon shone high and bright, casting a soft, muted glow from above.

"You don't approve of my wanting custody of Billy do you?" There was a distinctive challenge in her voice, and in her eyes. It fascinated him.

He lifted a finger to touch the curling ends of her hair. It was as soft as he'd imagined. "It's not a question of whether I approve or not. It's a question of what's right for Billy."

Annoyed, her temper flared. "And you don't think I've taken that into consideration?"

Aware he was touching the strands of her hair, she wanted to shift away from him, but found she couldn't. "I think that's really an arrogant assumption considering you don't even know me."

"Touché." He smiled, and something about that smile—it was lethally charming, incredibly potent, and ultimately male—made her far too nervous, and even more aware of him in spite of her aggravation. "But this is about Billy, not about you."

He considered for a moment, watching the way the amber glow of the porch light played on her features.

"Tell me something, Rina, exactly how much do you know about *Tin-ne-åh,* the Holy-Life Ways of The People?"

She stared at him blankly for a moment. "Apparently not enough since I'm not even sure I know what that means." His smile widened as if he'd proved a point, angering her.

"I...I..." She couldn't even begin to understand what he was talking about. "That doesn't mean I can't learn," she snapped with a defiant lift of her chin. "I'm a reasonably intelligent woman. There's absolutely no reason why I couldn't learn what I need in order to help Billy retain his culture."

He didn't think it wise to point out to her that there was no way she could learn about a culture, not the way Billy needed to live it, had lived it for most of his life.

"Would you like me to explain a bit about *Tin-ne-åh,* the Holy-Life Way of The People?" He waited for her nod, before continuing. "Billy is a descendant of the Teyas, a once powerful tribe of

Native Americans who are all but extinct now. There are probably only about a hundred or so of us left. Since Billy's one of the last descendants it's important that he carry on the traditions of the tribe. Not just for his sake, but for the tribe's sake. We've lost too many of our young people, and they in turn have lost their culture, their heritage. As the Shaman's grandson, Billy is a very important, very respected member of the tribe.''

"You mean they're all...gone?" Eyes wide, she shook her head, unable to comprehend that an entire race of people, an entire tribe, culture could be lost forever.

Hunter nodded. Feelings, emotions, loyalties churned inside him, making his eyes glow almost black.

He pointed off into the distance. "Past the Blackwell land, lies the Two Moon Reservation. It's Lipan, once thought to be descendants of the Teyas. Billy has spent his whole life on the reservation, learning and living *Tin-ne-åh*, the Holy-Life Way of The People. His people.''

She was certain he had a point with this, she just wasn't quite certain what that point was at the moment.

"And?" she prompted, searching his gaze. The look on his face made her set her teeth. "Do you think I don't know that Billy was born and raised on the reservation? Don't you think I know how important it is for Billy to learn and understand his culture and his people?" She sighed. "That's one of the reasons James decided to remain on the reservation, to stay here and teach, but also so that his son could have the benefit and the wisdom of his people.''

His gaze held hers, making her shiver. "If you know all of that, then tell me, do you really think it would be fair to yank Billy away from his home, from his family, from people who love him, and from a place where he is accepted and respected for who and what he is to start his life over again somewhere where he'll never belong in a world, a culture he really has no knowledge of?''

Thoughtfully, Rina's brows drew together. "That's ridiculous. Of course Billy will belong. He's my nephew, he's family.''

"I think you're being incredibly naive, Rina,'' Hunter said gently. "You have no idea how difficult it will be for Billy, and for others who will have a hard time accepting him for who he is simply because of his culture. In your world he'll always be…different.''

"That's ridiculous. In this day and age I can't believe that…'' Her voice trailed off, realizing he had a point. Worse, he was right. After James's sudden death, she'd been so shocked, so devastated, she hadn't paused to consider the enormous impact this would have on Billy. And his life.

The mere thought that someone—anyone— wouldn't be able to accept or respect her beloved nephew both angered and saddened her.

She'd been teaching long enough to have exposure to numerous multicultural students. She never, ever looked at their color, their race, or anything else for that matter. All she ever saw were kids...kids who needed her, kids who needed the knowledge she could teach them.

She shook her head in disbelief. "I can't believe that anyone would have a problem with my raising Billy." The sadness in her voice tugged at something deep inside of him.

Gently, Hunter caressed her shoulder, wanting to soothe the pain in her voice, the ache in her heart.

Because of tribal law she would never be permitted custody of Billy, nor would she ever be allowed to take the boy away from the reservation. He knew it, as did everyone else in town. Except for her, apparently.

Perhaps if he could get her to see and realize the hardships and prejudices both she and Billy would have to face she would be able to understand and accept the reality of the situation: that she'd never be allowed to have custody of Billy.

Perhaps if she understood this was for the best, it wouldn't devastate her.

Hunter looked at her, then sighed, realizing no matter how much he tried to reason, to explain, or to point out the obvious to her, when she realized the reality, that the tribe would never grant her custody of Billy, she was going to be hurt.

"Rina, have you thought of what you will do when you return to your home with a half-breed child?" His voice was soft. "What will your friends think? Do you think they will be so willing to accept a child who is not like them or one of them?''

Clenching her hands into impotent fists, Rina fought back tears, afraid she might not be able to hold on much longer. ''In the first place, anyone who would not accept my nephew is not my friend to begin with, regardless of his color or his culture.''

''And what about Billy?'' he asked softly, his gaze still on hers. ''What about Billy's feelings?'' he asked. ''What are you going to do when people talk and point and stare? And treat him as if he's some sideshow amusement simply because they've never met an Apache before?''

He couldn't stop the bitterness from lacing his words. It was too close to home, too painful.

''What then, Rina? How will you explain to Billy that even though he will never be able to fit into their culture—*your* culture—you took him away from his own culture, a place where he was accepted for exactly who he was, accepted and belonged, but you took him out of that environment simply because you thought it was best?'' He paused, letting his words sink in. ''You think taking Billy and raising him is best, but best for who, Rina?'' he asked quietly. ''Exactly who is this supposed to be best for?''

''He's...he's my nephew,'' she whispered impotently, tears slipping down her cheeks. At the moment, she couldn't seem to find the words to countermand his attack simply because she knew what he said was true. It was not a perfect world, no matter how much she wished it were.

"Billy's my only brother's child." She lifted her tear-stricken gaze to his. "I love him. I'm his family, too. He's all I have left."

Struck by her pain, Hunter pulled her close. Sniffling, Rina resisted only for a moment, then accepted the comfort he offered, laying her head on his shoulder. Pressed against him, she could hear the wild hammering of his heart against hers.

"I know," Hunter said quietly, stroking a hand down the silk of her hair, and wishing the fear and pain in her eyes, her heart, didn't move him so. But they did.

There was an aching vulnerability about her, and a sadness in her heart that words couldn't hide.

"But sometimes love is not enough to cover cultural biases and boundaries, especially when a vulnerable child is involved."

His natural mother's abandonment had devastated him on more levels than he'd ever truly begun to understand until he was an adult.

He didn't want the same thing to happen to Billy, and would do anything in his power to prevent it. For all their sakes.

"Trust me, I know," he said softly.

The tone of his voice caused Rina to look up at him. With his arm cradled around her, she was pressed against him from shoulder to waist. She could feel the hard wall of his chest. There was strength and stability there. And heat. So much heat, she felt warmed by it, drawn to it.

"What do you mean, you know?" With her eyes on his, she studied him. And then she saw the pain not even the depth of his eyes could hide. She laid a hand on his chest, wanting to soothe, to comfort. "Hunter, tell me. What happened?"

He sighed, covering her hand with his own, surprised anew at how delicate and small she was. "I'm a half-breed as well. My mother was white, my father Apache. She couldn't handle having a half-breed child."

"But why?" Suppressing her lips in frustration, Rina's gaze searched his. "That's ridiculous. How could a mother not love her own child?" The idea was so repugnant to her she couldn't even begin to comprehend it. Maybe because she'd always wanted children, longed for them, and just hadn't had the opportunity to have them.

He shook his head. "I don't know why she couldn't handle it." He blew out a breath. He couldn't remember the last time he'd talked about this with anyone but family. And he'd certainly never talked about it with a woman before. But for some reason, he felt comfortable confiding in Rina.

For Billy's sake, he assured himself. Only for Billy's sake.

"I don't remember much about her," he admitted hesitantly. He stared off somewhere into the distance, trying to ignore what the soft press of her body, her breasts pressed against him were doing to his system. "Just the beatings, the pain." His voice had dropped to a painful whisper. "When I was about five, I guess she couldn't take any more. One morning the Blackwells found me abandoned on the front porch." He brought his gaze back to hers. "Right there," he whispered, pointing.

Rina followed his gaze, feeling her stomach clench.

"Early one morning Justin and Emma Blackwell found me in that corner. Beaten, filthy, starving, and huddled in a ball like an animal." Rina snuggled closer, touched by the pain radiating in his voice.

He laughed softly, but the sound held no mirth. "I was so young, it's hard to remember much, except the fear. I remember being more frightened than I've ever been in my life. I sat huddled on that porch all night long. In the dark. I'd never been out all night by myself before."

Sometimes at night, even now, when the dark swooped in to turn the horizon black, he would dream of that long, lonely night, and the fear that had crept over him, cramping his little body, terrifying his five-year-old mind.

For years after, the dark had held unspeakable terrors. It was only his mother and father's love that had banished the terror, replacing it with love.

"Oh, my God." Snuggling closer, Rina wanted to hold him, to comfort, to erase the horror that filled her heart and her mind for what he'd been through. There was anger as well, at a mother who could be so cruel and so careless with her own precious child.

Hunter blew out a breath, trying to expel the tension that was tearing through him. Unconsciously, he tightened his arm around her, wanting, needing her closeness.

"The night seemed to go on forever. I was cold and hungry, and so unbearably scared. I must have dozed, but I don't remember. All I know is that it was suddenly light out. I looked up and saw Emma Blackwell standing there, holding out her hand to me." A smile softened his features. "I was absolutely certain she was an angel," he said quietly. He glanced down at her, stunned by how close she was. Her face, her mouth were just inches from his. And her eyes, those beautiful eyes were filled with something he didn't want to recognize, but couldn't resist.

Something strong, elemental, and more powerful than reason passed, sizzled between them.

Hunter's gaze dropped to her mouth. Her lips were soft, and so tantalizingly beckoning. It took all his willpower not to lower his mouth to hers, to take what he craved, wanted. Needed.

Shaken to his core by the feelings, needs and desires churning inside him, Hunter forced himself to glance away, then sighed, trying to rein in his control.

"The day the Blackwells found me was the luckiest day of my life. They took me in, gave me a home, a family, and more importantly, their love."

"Oh, Hunter." The tone in his voice almost broke her heart, and she snuggled closer, wanting to give him some of her warmth. To soothe and comfort the pain that he'd experienced as a child, the pain that was now so vividly apparent in the grown man.

"I'm so sorry," Rina said softly, aware that his closeness was making her heart rate accelerate, and doing incredible things to her pulse. "I don't understand a mother, any mother, abandoning or hurting her child. Any child," she clarified, aching for what he'd endured. "For any reason. Children are such a precious gift. To be cherished, loved, protected."

"I know," he whispered softly, surprised that her sentiments mirrored his own. "Perhaps because of what happened to me as a child…" He shrugged his massive shoulders. "Perhaps that's why I became a pediatrician."

"So that you could protect and care for children? To keep them safe, and unharmed?" He was a strong, principled man who had overcome devastating circumstances, using them to better himself, and others.

He nodded, stunned that she understood something he'd always had a hard time putting into words.

"Is that why you became a teacher?"

She nodded. "I've always loved kids. It just seemed so natural to me. That's why it's so important to me to raise Billy. To love him and show him he still has that one place." She stroked his chest. "I want to give Billy the same love and security the Blackwells gave you."

"This isn't a perfect world, Rina. People have

natural prejudices for whatever reason that they can't get past. And where Billy's concerned, those prejudices could be very detrimental to him.''

''But—''

''Rina, there's something I think you should know.'' It was time to tell her the truth; to let her know what she wanted to do was not possible. He couldn't allow himself to deceive her, or let her go on believing there was hope of taking Billy home with her, of gaining custody of him, or removing him from the reservation when there was none. It wouldn't be fair to her.

The tone of his voice had her tensing. ''What?'' She searched his gaze. ''What, Hunter? Please tell me.''

''Have you ever heard of the 1978 Federal Child Welfare Act?''

She shook her head, alarmed by the tone of his voice and the intensity of his gaze. ''No.'' She took a deep breath, trying to brace herself for what was to come. ''What is it?''

''It's a federal law that was passed to protect Indian children, to prevent them from being forcibly removed from the reservations to be adopted by white families.''

''Wait a minute.'' She closed her eyes, and took a deep breath, trying to sort out all the things he was telling her. ''I thought…I thought…you told me that you were adopted by the Blackwells?'' This wasn't making sense. ''If you were part Native American, then how could they adopt you?'' She shook her head, trying to understand. "I thought they were white."

"They are. But I was adopted in 1960, eighteen years before the Federal Child Welfare Act took effect." He sighed. "Before the federal law was passed, Native American children were being taken from the reservations by whites who couldn't have children of their own. It led to a very unhealthy situation. The children were being torn from their homes, their families and their traditions, thrust into a world and a culture that couldn't or wouldn't accept them." He shrugged, his words bearing the bitterness he still felt. "A lot of times, when it didn't work out, when the Indian children weren't accepted in the traditional white world, they were beaten, abused and even abandoned by the people who were supposed to love and care for them."

Her gaze, frantic and fearful, searched his. She knew now why he had told her of his own childhood, his own past.

"Are you saying that Billy's grandfather is prepared to take legal action to retain custody of Billy?" The mere thought nearly brought on a bout of panic. As soon as she'd learned of her brother's death, and not knowing how long it would take to take care of all the legalities of Billy's custody, she'd left her job, her home, everything so that she could come to Texas. With her credentials, she was absolutely certain obtaining another teaching position wouldn't be difficult.

But now, she realized leaving her job might have

been premature. With no income, and a small bit of savings, how on earth could she take on a lengthy, and no doubt costly legal battle for custody of her nephew? The mere thought left her feeling ill.

"Billy's grandfather doesn't have to take legal action to keep or retain custody of Billy," Hunter said.

Fearful and frustrated, Rina fought the lump that had formed in her throat. "I don't understand."

He sighed. He hadn't realized his own emotions would make this so difficult. "Rina, the Apache are a matriarchal tribe. Children belong to their mother's family."

"But Billy's mother is dead!"

"Yes," he said patiently, "but that merely means that Billy now belongs to the tribe. His mother's people."

"But that's ridiculous." She tried to pull away from him, but he tightened his arm around her shoulder, not wanting to let her go. Not now. Not when he knew she was hurting, and he was the cause. "How can a whole tribe have custody of one child? That's ridiculous."

"Perhaps. But that's not just the law, but the way of The People. And in this case, that means that a tribal court will automatically grant custody of Billy to his mother's father. In this case his grandfather, the Shaman."

"Are you saying I won't even be considered for custody?" She could almost feel her hope and her heart shatter. "That I don't stand a chance of getting custody?'' Her fingers clutched the material of his shirt as she fought back tears. "Hunter, this not only doesn't make sense, but isn't even practical. Surely the court has to take into consideration his grandfather's age and health?" She paused to take a breath, struggling not to cry. "I mean, really, anyone with any common sense has to see that in his grandfather's fragile state of health he's not physically capable of raising a child, especially a confused, rebellious teenager. I know they have a special relationship, and I respect that, I truly do, but clearly they have to see that perhaps Billy's grandfather is not capable of raising him."

"It's not a question of whether his grandfather is physically capable of raising him or not, Rina. It's simply a matter of tribal law. And you have to remember," he added softly, "in our culture, we value and respect our elders for their knowledge and their wisdom."

"Are you telling me that I don't have a prayer in hell of gaining custody of Billy?"

He sighed. "Yes, I'm afraid that's exactly what I'm telling you. You cannot take Billy from the reservation, nor can you take him away from his grandfather or the tribe."

"Oh, God." Tears scalded her eyes and Rina surged to her feet to pace the length of the porch. "Hunter, that's...that's...ridiculous, and so unfair."

"Billy is half Apache. You must never forget that," he said patiently.

"How can I?" she demanded, fury quickening

her steps as she continued to pace the porch. "What you're telling me is that you don't want me to ignore his Apache heritage, his culture, but you expect me to ignore my part of his heritage."

He didn't realize until this moment that what she said made sense. At least to her; he was certain.

"No, Rina, that's not what I'm saying. There's no law that says you can't be part of his life."

"How am I going to be part of his life from Chicago?" she cried, dragging a hand through her hair in frustration. He forced himself to meet her gaze, troubled by the sadness and fear he saw reflected in her eyes. "What you're saying is that even if Billy is half white, the fact that he's half Apache is more important?" Sniffling, she swiped at her nose with the back of her hand.

"Not more important," he clarified slowly. "But *as* important."

She disagreed, but at the moment, didn't see any point in making her feelings known.

She met his gaze, blinking away tears. "And this law, this Child Welfare Act says that no matter what, I can't have custody of my brother's son? That I can't be part of his life, his family?" The tears came faster then, and she didn't even bother to try to stop them.

It was a double loss and tore at her fragile heart. It was far too much for her to handle in her current state. She'd lost her brother and her nephew all in the same week. Once again she felt all alone, and totally helpless.

It wasn't fair. Not fair at all.

"Oh, God," she moaned, desperation etching her words.

Not wanting him to see her tears, she whirled away from him, leaning against the porch, shutting her eyes against the pain and frustration that was tearing her heart apart.

"Rina." He laid a large, warm hand on her back. "I'm sorry," he said softly.

She whirled to him, surprised to find him standing right behind her, so close she almost bumped into him.

"Are you?" she challenged, meeting his gaze with her own tear-filled one. "Are you really sorry?" She didn't give him a chance to answer. "You're a doctor, Hunter. If you were really sorry, you'd see that the Shaman is not physically capable of raising Billy."

Torn by her tears, her pain, he slid his hands to her waist. "Don't cry, Rina," he whispered. "Remember, this is not about what we want, but what's best for Billy. And there's no way I would ever agree that taking Billy from the reservation, from his grandfather or The People would be best for him."

She didn't want to hear any more. She simply couldn't bear it. She tried to step around him, but his hands, so large, so warm, so gentle, tightened on her waist.

"Hunter—please." She lifted her chin, her eyes

glimmering with tears, stunned by how close he was, and how much he was affecting her.

He agreed with this law, agreed that she shouldn't be allowed to raise her nephew. So how could she be responding to him like this?

She laid a hand to her speeding heart, wondering how she could be feeling so many emotions at once, emotions that were racing through her, angering her, exciting her.

She tilted her chin, met his gaze, and felt her heart skip. The warmth of his body, the heat of his hands were wreaking havoc on her body, her mind, her emotions.

In spite of her anger, her pain, she knew from the look on his face, in his eyes, what he wanted to do, what she longed for him to do, what she'd craved from the moment she'd laid eyes on him.

He was holding her gently, protectively. It made her aching heart ache even more.

"Rina." He lifted a hand, and laid it along her cheek. With his thumb he brushed aside a tear. "Don't cry. This isn't a war between us. It's merely what's best for Billy. You have to remember that."

He slid his arms around her, letting his hands warm and caress her back. Through the thin material of her shirt, she could feel his heat, his gentleness, and she couldn't help but respond as he pulled her closer, until they were pressed together.

"N-no. Please." She lifted a hand to his chest to keep him at bay. "This can't...happen." His head was lowering, coming closer and closer. "We...

can't...do this...we—'' His mouth stopped her words. Filled with hunger and need, desire flared so hot, so quickly, she was absolutely certain it would incinerate them both.

His mouth was soft, gentle, giving, but she gave in return, stunned by the impact the touch of his lips had on her.

For an instant it felt as if someone had tilted the porch floor, sending her spiraling into orbit. With a muffled groan, she slid her arms around him, wanting to bring him closer, then closer still as she clutched at the back of his shirt, trying to hang on from being drawn into a whirlpool that had her legs weakening and her thoughts scrambling.

Hunter pulled her closer until he could feel the softness of her unbound breasts pressing enticingly against his chest. He could feel her nipples harden as he gently slid his tongue between her lips, wanting to sip, to savor, to lose himself in her.

Her mouth opened under his, and she rose on tiptoe, wanting, needing more of him. His taste, his scent, his body. Everything that was female in her responded to him, to his maleness, wanting to lose herself in him the way a drowning man loses himself in a stream.

His hand stroked the length of her back, sliding to the gentle curve of her buttocks, pulling her closer, pressing his hardness against her. With a soft moan of unbridled desire, she pressed closer to him, wanting to ease the ache in her body, her heart.

Her breasts ached, her nipples puckered, begging

for attention. When his large hand moved from her back to cup her breast, she moaned, and his open mouth caught it, dragging her deeper into the sea of desire. She wrapped her arms tighter around him, stunned by the desire that had flared to life the moment he had touched her, kissed her.

For the first time in her life, Rina understood the need to mate, to be one, to want a man to fill all the empty spaces in her life, her heart, her body. It stunned her for she'd never known she was capable of such feelings, such passions, such needs.

Hunter's touch had awakened and exploded all the unfulfilled desire that had been lying dormant for so many years.

Dragging her closer, wanting more, Hunter heard the distant clanging of a warning, but ignored it. This need, this desire was far stronger, causing him to forget all the lessons he had learned, all the lessons he'd vowed never to forget when it came to a woman.

Rina was soft, warm, welcoming, igniting like a smoldering fire from his touch. All that was male in him responded, wanting to quench that fire with his own, unwilling to listen to his mind when his heart was filled with such yearning.

"Hunter..." Rina's whispered moan brought him to his senses, and he immediately withdrew from her, stunned that he'd allowed this to happen.

With her.

He was older, smarter, and he'd thought wiser.

Too old and far too wise to let his emotions or his testosterone rule his intellect.

"I'm sorry." Dragging shaky hands through his hair, he took a deep breath. "I'm sorry," he said again.

Hurt by his abrupt dismissal, and the fact that he'd expressed sorrow for something that had been so beautiful—at least to her—Rina felt her temper rise.

"And just what exactly are you sorry for, Hunter?" His head came up; his eyes glittered as they met hers. "Are you sorry you kissed me? Or are you sorry for wanting me?"

There was silence for a moment. "Both," he said quietly, knowing he wasn't sorry for kissing her, and wanting to do it again. Now.

He took a step back so that he wouldn't do something foolish, trying to remember that he could not get involved with this woman.

Too late, his mind echoed, but he refused to acknowledge the truth.

"Is it because I'm not..." Hurt and still shaken, Rina had to swallow in order to continue. Her lips still ached from his kiss, her breasts still tingled from his touch. "Are you sorry because I'm white?"

"No," he lied, feeling small. "It's because of Billy." He dragged his hands through his hair again, wishing he'd taken up smoking. Anything that would help ease this tension that was tearing through him at the moment would be welcome.

He dipped his hands into his pockets so he wouldn't reach for her again. "This situation...I don't...'' He was stammering like a twelve-year-old, he realized, feeling like a fool. It was just that he wasn't accustomed to lying. ''You don't know anything about The People. About me. About my life.''

''I could learn,'' she said quietly. ''I need to learn,'' she admitted, watching him slowly withdraw from her, and trying not to let it hurt. But it did. ''If I'm going to be part of Billy's life I need to learn about that life.'' She laid a hand to his heart, wanting, needing to touch him. His heart was thudding as recklessly as hers. Somehow it pleased her to know he'd been as affected as she by their encounter. ''Will you teach me, Hunter?'' Her gaze, soft and serious searched his. ''Will you teach me about...*Tin-ne-åh,* the Holy Life-Way of The People?'' She took a deep breath. ''Please, Hunter. It's important to me. Very important. I need to know, to learn.'' She'd do anything to prove that she was indeed capable of raising Billy. And if that meant learning about his culture, his way of life, she would do it. Surely then, the powers that be would have to see that his grandfather was too old and ill to care for him; that she was the only logical choice.

It was a small possibility, but one she had to take. What other choice did she have?

Did he dare? Hunter wondered, knowing if he agreed he would have difficulty keeping her at a distance, both physically and emotionally.

Could he risk it? he wondered.

More importantly, was he strong enough now to resist the lure she presented, and the danger she represented, not just to the tribe, to Billy, to Hunter's life, but to his aching, battered heart?

The feelings she aroused in him were so powerful they frightened him.

"Will you, Hunter? Teach me. Please?" She clutched his shirt tighter, wanting to drag him closer, but not daring. "Until the Shaman and Billy come back, I really don't have anything to do. It's the perfect time and opportunity. What have you got to lose?"

More than she could ever imagine, he suddenly realized. He had far too much at stake. His promise to the Shaman, his responsibility to Billy...and his heart.

He sighed deeply, letting his emotions overrule his intellect. He knew he should back off and away from this woman. To just walk away and let her fight and fend for herself. Agreeing to help her would be like undermining his own intentions.

But he wasn't a man who had ever walked away from someone in need.

And he knew she was in need. Of Billy. And of what he could teach her about their ways and their people.

Perhaps it was wrong, but knowing that the courts would not bend on this—ever—he realized that teaching her their ways could do no harm, and might just help her to understand why it was so important for Billy to remain with his people.

"Yes, Rina," he said with a weary sigh, saying a silent prayer that the Spirits of Mischief would be busy elsewhere. And that the Spirits of Protection would walk with him on this journey. For something about this woman drew him like no other before. And it frightened him on too many levels, but he was not a man who allowed fear to rule his life. Not anymore.

His gaze met hers, and his arms tightened around her, drawing her close until her head rested on the wall of his chest. "I will help you to learn about the Holy Life-Way of The People."

And he would protect himself and his heart, he promised, wondering if it was too late already.

He kissed the top of her head, letting her sweet, feminine scent tease him.

Yes, he would protect himself.

Or try to.

And at least it would give him something to do with her until the Shaman and Billy returned.

He just hoped they'd return...soon.

Chapter Five

Over the next several days, two things became quite clear to Rina. Her idea of *soon* and Hunter's were obviously not the same, since she hadn't heard a word from Billy or the Shaman.

Nor did Hunter have any idea how *soon* they would return.

"Rina," Hunter told her repeatedly. "You have to understand. This process of accepting his parents' deaths will not be an easy one for Billy. He needs whatever time necessary to come to peace with this situation. You must not worry or rush these things. Billy's welfare must come first."

And so she'd stopped worrying about when Billy and his grandfather would return, assuring herself that however long it took, it was for Billy's own good. Besides, she would make good use of the time in order to help her cause of getting custody of her nephew.

The second thing Rina discovered as Hunter attempted to teach and show her *Tin-ne-åh:* The Holy-Life Way of The People was that he was either trying to scare her off...or wear her out.

She was absolutely positive she'd walked every square inch of the reservation, which, in her estimation had to be close to seventy-five acres.

She'd eaten something called fry bread and eagle stew, which Hunter assured her was minus the eagle—although the mischief in his eyes at the time he said it didn't go a long way toward reassuring her of anything.

They'd stood in the moonlight, watching as the big black kettle bubbled over the huge fire that had been started in a deep hole in the ground.

The wonderful aroma cascaded through the night air, perfuming it with a mixture of spices that were strange, and yet so wonderful they almost made her swoon.

Surrounded by several tribal families who did their best to make her feel welcome, Rina sat cross-legged on the ground, ate her stew out of a blue cast-iron plate, and listened to stories from the elder men of the tribe, as they spun legends about the past that fascinated and amazed her.

And everywhere she went, everyone was kind to her, saying wonderful things about her brother James without actually saying his name because to actually speak the name of the dead was to tempt the Spirits of Evil.

She had no idea how many people her brother had known, or touched. Nor had she had any idea how much Billy was cared for.

One night Hunter had taken her up to a ridge high above the reservation, and they had sat for hours in the moonlight, talking, listening, and watching the sights and sounds of life and nature unfold down below.

There was an ancient beauty about the slow-paced life on the reservation, about the way people did things in a manner they had been doing them for hundreds of years. It was like watching a living tradition unfold before her eyes. She was absolutely certain she'd never appreciated the natural beauty of life until that moment.

During the past several days, she and Hunter had spent hours and hours together. She went with him on his rounds at the hospital in the city, and then went with him to the tribal clinic, watching as he soothed mothers and tended to sick or injured babies.

She'd marveled at his expertise, his knowledge, but more importantly, she marveled and admired his convictions, his dedication, and more than anything else, his overwhelming kindness.

At the tribal clinic, she knew it was a rare occasion for him to be paid in anything more than sweet cakes or cornmeal, but he never complained, and showered praise and thanks on whoever pressed whatever into his hand for payment.

And he'd meant it.

She'd marveled and admired, but more than anything else, Rina found herself drawn more and more to this man who had a depth of kindness she hardly believed possible, not just for his own people, but for all people. Young and old. Rich or poor.

And always, especially for the children he cared for.

One night, late into the night, she'd sat in the hospital waiting room while he comforted one of the elders of the tribe, holding his hand long into the night so he wouldn't be alone when the Death Spirit came to him.

When it was over, Hunter had been dazed and drained, and clearly shaken by the death of another of the elders.

She wanted to soothe, to comfort, to hold him until the lines of worry and fatigue eased his brow, but she didn't, simply because the more she got to know Hunter, the harder it was to control and contain her growing feelings for him.

She fought it, tried to deny it, but as each day passed, Rina realized she was drawn more and more to Hunter. Her feelings grew, deepening day by day.

Shortly before dawn on this morning, Hunter shook her awake with the news that he wanted to take her somewhere.

Groggy with sleep, she stumbled out of bed and into the shower, and then slipped into her clothes, before going down the stairs bleary eyed, to find Sadie standing in the kitchen, holding out a steaming cup of coffee to her.

"Bless you," Rina mumbled, making Sadie laugh as she downed the coffee, not bothering to wince even though she was certain the coffee had scalded the first layer of her tongue off.

She needed caffeine and lots of it if she was going to stay upright.

"Where are we going?" Rina finally asked Hunter, when her eyes seemed as if they would finally stay open without toothpicks. It annoyed her that the man was so bright-eyed and gorgeous at this ungodly hour of the morning.

"To a sacred place," he said simply. "A place you should know."

She nodded as if that was all the explanation she needed. And it was.

After downing half of a second cup of coffee, and grabbing the oversize sweatshirt Sadie held out to her, she followed Hunter out to his truck.

The sweatshirt had to belong to Hunter or one of his brothers she realized as she slipped it over her head, and found it hanging nearly to her knees.

"Try to go back to sleep," he said as he started the engine. "It's going to take a couple of hours to get there."

Too tired to argue, she closed her eyes, tucked up her legs, and snuggled into a ball, falling fast asleep.

It wasn't until Hunter shook her shoulder, and

gently brushed the sleep-tousled hair from her face that she realized the truck had stopped.

Waking slowly, she covered a yawn, stretched her legs, then smiled at Hunter, gratefully accepting the thermos of coffee he offered her.

"Where are we?" she asked, finishing the steaming coffee and blessing Sadie once again.

"There's someone I wanted you to meet." After relieving her of the thermos cup, he pushed another tangle of hair off her face and gently kissed her lips.

Blinking, Rina closed her eyes and gave in to the sensations swamping her. With a sigh, she lifted her arms around him, drawing him closer, aware that what had started as a quick, friendly kiss had suddenly turned into something hot and dangerous.

A sigh escaped her mouth as she felt the first glorious touch of his clever tongue, wanting, aching for more as he quickly dragged her into that unknown abyss of passion.

Her body trembled with need, desire. Her heart was racing, slamming into her rib cage long before his large, gentle hand covered it, to tease and entice.

The touch of his hand on her breast, the feel of his finger stroking her nipple caused her body to throb and ache. She arched against him, moaning softly, no longer frightened by the intense feelings he aroused.

Her fingers slid, then tangled through the glorious strands of his hair, dragging him still closer, wanting more of him, wanting only to assuage the sudden ache of desire and need that his kiss and his touch had aroused.

When his hand slid under her sweatshirt, skin to skin, warmth to warmth, to stroke, to caress, to tease until she was moaning softly, arching against him to get closer, the world seemed to dip and tilt again until there was nothing in it but him and his touch.

"Oh, Rina," the softly muttered words were either a curse or a prayer. Stunned by the impact Rina was having on him, Hunter groaned softly, knowing he had to stop now or he wouldn't be able to. He slowly retreated, reluctantly drawing his mouth from hers, knowing he had no right in hell to be doing this, to be touching her, or allowing her to invade his heart, or his mind.

Too late, a small voice protested. He ignored it, knowing he was treading on very dangerous ground.

The past few days, the more time they spent together, the more time he wanted to spend with her. He was becoming attached, emotionally and physically in a way he'd never been before.

And it scared the daylights out of him considering his history with women.

But not enough to stay away from her.

He couldn't, he realized. The desire he felt for her, the need to possess her in the way a man possessed a woman was making him lose his concentration, forget his purpose, lose his peace.

And he knew from experience how dangerous that could be.

He released her, but kept one hand on her back,

unwilling to break all contact with that soft, feminine body.

Rina's small groan of protest almost had him reaching for her again. But he resisted—barely. To lighten the mood and to get his breathing and his body under control, he kissed her nose, then her forehead, trying to ignore the needs that were roiling inside him.

"Hunter…" Rina said, staring at him.

In the tension-filled silence of the car, the shriek of a bird startled her, and she jumped, glancing around. "You know, the first couple of days after I arrived I jumped every time I heard one of those birds."

"I know," he said with a laugh. "The first time you heard a hawk, you screeched so loud, you almost scared me out of my shoes." He caressed her sleep-warmed cheek.

"Now, I've gotten used to it."

Hunter sighed, glancing at the horizon, enjoying the beautiful sight. "I always wonder if I'll ever get tired of the beauty and the sights and sounds out here." He turned back to look at her. "But I never do. Each one seems precious, like a mysterious gift from the Great Spirit." He smiled. "Come on, I want you to meet someone." He caught her hand, tugging her out of the truck behind him.

"Watch your step," he cautioned, using her hand for leverage to draw her closer until he could slide a hand around her slender waist. "The ground is rocky and uneven up here, and not packed real well. It might shift.''

That brought her to an abrupt halt, causing Hunter to turn and look at her with that mischievous look in his eyes. ''What?'' he asked, trying not to smile.

''The ground's not packed and might shift?'' she repeated, her voice edging upward in panic, making him smile.

''What? Are you worried?'' he teased, tugging her closer, and giving her a quick hug simply because she did look so worried. ''Don't worry, Rina.'' He laughed, letting her go because he knew having her close enough to reach for was far too dangerous.

''You're safe with me.'' He pushed her hair off her cheeks again as the soft wind caught it, sending it cascading around her face. ''Don't you trust me?''

''You, I trust,'' she commented, with a frown. ''It's the ground that's worrying me,'' she said skeptically. ''I'm not very adept at flying. Yet,'' she added with a grin, tightening her hand on his.

''Come on.'' He tugged her along. She could see that he'd driven the truck high up on the canyons of the reservation. When he'd reached a crest almost at the top of a bluff, he stopped and turned to her, pointing. ''What do you see?''

She glanced around her, then down...and felt her stomach nearly rise into her throat. Her eyes slid closed for a moment.

''Hunter,'' she said on a shaky breath, blindly reaching for him. ''Did I happen to mention this little fear of heights I have?'' Automatically, she took a step back.

He laughed, dropping an arm around her shoulder so she'd feel safer. ''Only about a hundred times in the past few days.''

''We're up...high.'' She swallowed, unwilling to open her eyes.

He grinned, grabbing a handful of her sweatshirt from the back, and reining her in closer just to make certain she didn't go anywhere. ''Yes, I know.''

''So why did you drag me out of bed at the crack of dawn?'' She opened her eyes to peek at him. ''To scare the dickens out of me?''

He laughed. ''No. Look.'' He pointed again, and he realized she'd have to open her eyes to look at the lone house in the distance, and the woman who sat in front of it.

''What is that?'' Rina asked as she glanced to where he pointed.

''Not a what, Rina,'' he assured her. ''A who. It's a who.''

''Okay,'' she agreed. ''Then who is it?'' He'd grabbed her hand and started walking again in the direction of the who.

''It's Mary,'' he said with a smile, and from the affection in his voice she had a feeling whoever Mary was, she was someone important. ''Come on, let's go see Mary. Don't worry, it's not that far.''

''I remember the last time you told me that,'' she grumbled, holding his hand tightly as he led her down the bluff toward the woman. "I think we walked twenty miles that day."

One of the things that had surprised Rina about the reservation, was not just its vastness, but its varying terrains and altitudes.

In some places, on the flat ground, where the majority of the tribe lived, cars were parked and scattered about.

But as you climbed or walked higher up the bluffs, driving was impossible. You could only drive so far, and then you had to leave your car and walk wherever it was that you were going.

Huffing and puffing as Hunter tugged her along, keeping up a running monologue along the way so she wouldn't worry about how high they were, no doubt, Rina realized how quiet, how peaceful, how *happy* she was.

As they finally approached the other side of the bluff, Rina could see the small house more clearly.

In front of the house sat an old woman, with a sun-creased face, and gnarled hands who lovingly weaved a basket, humming a song in a sweet, cheerful voice.

"Who is she?" Rina had whispered, fascinated.

"That's Mary," Hunter said, pulling her close to whisper in her ear. "She doesn't speak much English, and she's not comfortable around many strangers, so just stand there and stand still, so she can get a good look at you."

"Stand there and stand still," she repeated, glancing in the woman's direction.

"And don't stare," he cautioned, turning her chin so Rina was looking up at him and not Mary. "In our culture it's considered rude to stare."

She rolled her eyes, suddenly aware of how many times he'd caught her staring. At him. Oh, Lord.

"And you didn't think it was important to tell me before this?"

He laughed again, brushing her hair back off her face and giving her another quick kiss for courage. "Mary will like your hair." He touched it almost reverently, making her wish he wouldn't do it, simply because it always made her knees weak when he touched her.

"Why?" she asked with a frown.

"Because it's the color of fire, and because it's long. Mary is very traditional and believes a woman's strength, her power and her beauty are in her hair."

"Strength and power," she said with a grin as he started tugging her along toward Mary. "Guess I'll have to remember that."

Mary looked up from her weaving and the moment she saw Hunter, she gave him a big, toothless smile, getting to her feet to give him a ferocious hug, before saying something in her native tongue that had Hunter laughing.

Rina followed him simply because curiosity dictated it. After Mary finished hugging Hunter, standing on tiptoe to hold his face gently in her hands so she could kiss both his cheeks, his eyes, and then his forehead, she turned her attention to Rina who stood stock-still, as instructed, and waited. Not looking at the woman. Definitely not looking at the woman.

Although she badly wanted to.

The sun had finally awakened, and was bathing the earth with heat and light. Trying not to fidget, Rina glanced at Hunter as Mary slowly circled her, speaking in her native tongue as she did. Mary reached out once, to touch her hair, and smiled, obviously pleased.

"She wants to know if the Spirit of Fire has visited you?" Hunter translated Mary's question for Rina, then answered Mary in his native tongue.

He laughed suddenly, as Mary said something else.

"What did she say?" Rina whispered.

"She said that you have skin the color of the moon, and hair touched by the Spirit of Fire, but you obviously need a good meal."

"Great. You make me sound like Howdy Doody," she said with a laugh, trying to look everywhere but at Mary.

Her inspection finished, Mary finally came to a halt in front of Rina and opened her arms. Touched, Rina glanced at Hunter for one quick moment, before being enfolded in the older woman's embrace.

Mary smelled of the sun and the earth...and goodness. That was the only word Rina could think of as she hugged the woman back, touched by the motherly gesture.

She spent the morning watching, and then eventually helping Mary as Hunter went to feed her stock, water her crops and plants, and chop wood for Mary's fire.

Content, Rina sat on a chair, rocking in much the same way Mary did, as the old woman patiently showed her with words and gestures, how to weave a basket.

"She's the Wedding Weaver," Hunter explained, when he came back.

"What's a Wedding Weaver?" Rina asked.

"It's said when the Spirit of Love descends on a male, when he's told of the woman that's his destiny, he comes to see Mary, the Wedding Weaver, for a marriage basket."

"And?" Rina prompted when she feared he wouldn't continue. Hunter went down on his haunches, fingering one of the many baskets that sat on the ground.

"Then the intended groom fills the marriage basket with gifts for the bride's family."

Rina grinned. "I think I like this tradition. So what kinds of gifts are we talking about here?"

Hunter shrugged. "Gifts from the earth. Fruits, berries, corn. In the old days, sometimes he even offered his horse." He gave her a mischievous smile. "That was only when he was really pleased with the woman the Love Spirit chose for him."

Rina frowned, trying to understand. "And so how does the guy know when and who the Love Spirit has chosen?"

"They say he is struck by a feeling, a knowledge

and wisdom that cannot be defined.'' Like what Hunter felt when he held *her,* touched her. No, his mind echoed. Don't even go there. Too dangerous. Too treacherous. This woman wasn't for him. Stunned by his own thoughts, Hunter glanced down at a basket, touching the weaving. ''They say when a man looks at a woman, the right woman, the one the Love Spirit has destined for him, he will know it.''

Rina stared at him, stunned. ''What happens if the Love Spirit never makes the choice known?''

Hunter laughed. ''Then the guy remains a lonely, old bachelor.'' He grinned. ''Like me.''

''So are you saying the Love Spirit never chose a woman for you?'' There was a challenge in her voice, daring him to deny what was obviously happening between them.

He thought carefully about his answer. ''I figure he's been too busy to bother.'' He stood, stretching under the warmth of the sun, uncomfortable with the topic simply because his own feelings and emotions about Rina were as tangled and confused as the basket she'd been attempting to weave all morning. ''Besides, I told you I'm too busy with my practice to have time for anything else in my life. Especially a woman.''

His words hurt, but pride would not let Rina show it. Instead, she concentrated on her weaving, deliberately ignoring Hunter, the topic, and the ache in her heart his words had brought on.

It seemed as if she spent hours weaving her basket, concentrating, making mistakes, but trying nonetheless. Although her basket didn't look quite as good as Mary's, the morning passed pleasantly into afternoon.

Patiently, Mary guided Rina's hands, slowly, lovingly showing her the gentle strokes, the different weaves that gave each basket its distinctive look.

After a lunch of fry bread and another kind of stew cooked over an open fire that Hunter had built, they were just settling back to continue weaving when Hunter's beeper went off.

"I'll be right back." Pulling out his portable phone, Hunter walked around the back of the small house, and returned a moment later. "Rina, I'm sorry. We've got to go. There's an emergency at the tribal clinic." He went to Mary and placed a hand on her shoulder, explaining to her that they were leaving, and why.

She said something back to him that made him smile. "Mary says to leave your basket. That you will come back again so she can help you finish it and teach you more."

Getting to her feet, Rina lovingly set the lopsided basket on her rocking chair. "Tell her I'd like that."

Hunter did, and this time, not waiting for Mary, Rina went to the woman and gave her a hug, whispering her thanks.

"You're welcome," Mary whispered back in English, surprising Rina. A look passed between them. "The young ones, they expect tradition." Grinning a toothless grin, Mary shrugged. "So I give them tradition.'' Her English was far from perfect, but clear enough for Rina to understand.

"Thank you," she said softly, giving Mary another hug, touched beyond measure by what the woman had showed her, shared with her. "You've been very kind."

Mary took her by the arms, then stood on tiptoe to kiss her cheeks, her eyes, then her forehead, much the same way she had done to Hunter when they'd arrived.

After bidding farewell to Mary, and hugging her with a promise they'd return soon, Hunter grabbed Rina's hand and started hustling toward the car.

"Hunter," she said, pressing a hand to her racing heart. "I know this is an emergency, but if you don't slow down, you're going to have another emergency on your hands. Me."

"Sorry." He slowed his pace. "But Beth Anne said Joey Whitecloud's mother called. She was so hysterical, Beth Anne couldn't get much out of her except that something was wrong with her Joey." He sighed. "Again. So they're on their way to the clinic."

"Sounds like you're familiar with Joey Whitecloud."

"Very," Hunter said with a smile. "His grandfather is one of the most respected tribal judges on the reservation. Now Joey, well..." Hunter laughed. "Joey's the personification of the terrible twos carried over into age four. If there's mischief, there's a good bet little Joey's in the middle of it. He's driving his mother and grandfather crazy." He shook his head. "I can't imagine what he's done this time. Something inspired, no doubt." He looked at Rina. "The kid's only four. I hate to see what he's going to be like when he's ten."

In spite of her racing heart, Rina quickened her pace. Even though Hunter was treating this lightly, she saw the worry in his eyes, on his face. "Once we get to the truck, how long will it take us to get to the tribal clinic?"

"About ten or fifteen minutes depending on traffic and how good your nerves are," he said with that mischievous smile of his.

It turned out it only took them ten minutes. By the time Hunter's truck screeched to a halt in front of the clinic and he jumped out, they could hear the wails of a little boy coming from inside.

The waiting room was empty, since it was Wednesday, and the clinic was technically closed except for emergencies Hunter explained, or if a child was sick, hurt or injured.

"Where is he?" Hunter asked, placing a comforting arm on Joey's mother as she wrung her hands together and cried in Hunter's office. She was young and frail-looking in spite of her advanced state of pregnancy.

"Your...your nurse took him."

He patted her shoulder. "What can you tell me, Margaret?"

The mother's eyes welled and she placed a protective hand over her stomach. "Not much, Dr.

Blackwell. Joey was out back, playing with his friends. The next thing I knew, he came running into the house, holding his nose, and crying.''

"His nose?" Hunter repeated. "Was he bleeding? Bruised? Are there any marks on him?" As he spoke, Hunter began moving toward his examining room down the hall. He stopped when he realized Joey's mother and Rina were following him. "Wait here," he said, giving Rina a look that she quickly understood. He couldn't handle an injured child and a crying mother.

"Come on," Rina said, draping an arm around the woman and steering her back around toward the waiting room. "Let's wait back here so Dr. Blackwell can tend to Joey." She pulled a clean, but crumpled tissue from her pocket, handing it the woman with a smile. "It won't do Joey any good to see you crying. It will probably just scare him."

Nodding, the woman took the tissue, wiped her eyes, swiped at her nose, and slumped heavily into a chair.

"When are you due?" Rina asked, taking the seat next to her and hoping to make small talk to keep the woman's mind off her child, who was now wailing and screaming in earnest.

She smiled, patting her stomach. "In six weeks. The Shaman and Dr. Blackwell are going to deliver the baby."

Considering this news—that Hunter delivered babies along with everything else—Rina was proud of herself. She only managed to gape at the woman for a moment.

"They delivered Joey as well." The young mother laughed. "I should have known after the childbirth I had that boy was going to be a handful."

Rina smiled. "Are you hoping for a girl?"

With a sigh, the woman closed her eyes. "If the Spirits are as wise as I think they are, they'll gift me with two girls." She sighed, pushing her short cropped hair off her forehead. "One male child has about done me in."

The wailing and crying came to an abrupt halt, and Joey's mother jumped to her feet when Hunter appeared with a red-eyed toddler in his arms, sucking on a lollipop.

"He's fine," Hunter said, passing the child to his mother, who expertly tucked him onto her hip.

"What was wrong with him?" She examined her son with her eyes and a hand in the way only a mother can do; a mother who knows every inch of her child, and instinctively knows anytime anything is wrong even if she doesn't know exactly *what's* wrong.

Hunter grinned, dragging a hand through his hair. "Corn kernels," he said, trying not to look amused.

Joey's mother looked at him blankly. As did Rina. "Corn kernels?" Margaret looked down at her son, whose eyes were drooping now because of his tears. "He was crying because of corn kernels?" She shook her head. "Why?"

Hunter's smile bloomed. "Because he'd stuffed a batch of them up his nose."

Rina couldn't help it, she started to laugh, then muffled her mouth with her hand when Joey lifted his head to stare at her in curiosity.

"Up his nose?" Joey's mother repeated in horror, rolling her eyes toward the skies. She looked at Rina. "The Spirits better grant me a reprieve. That's all I can say. Two females," she reiterated, turning her attention back to Hunter. "Is he going to be okay?" There was a hint of exasperation in her tone overlaid by bemusement.

Hunter nodded. "He'll be fine. I retrieved the kernels, then bathed the inside of his nasal cavity with some antiseptic to prevent infection and to soothe the irritation." He tousled Joey's black hair. "He's going to be sore and probably a bit cranky for the rest of the day, so I think you'd better keep an eye on him."

"This child is not leaving my sight." She planted a loud, smacking kiss on her son's cheek, making the child grin sleepily. "Until he's thirty," she added with enough emphasis to make Hunter and Rina believe her.

Rubbing his brow, Hunter tried not to laugh. "Perhaps the next time Joey gets a hankering for some corn, it should be on his plate."

Smiling in gratitude, the woman stood on tiptoe and kissed Hunter. "Thank you Dr. Blackwell. I don't know what we'd do without you."

"You're welcome. Don't forget, keep an eye on Joey today—"

"I'm putting him down for a nap the minute we get home," Joey's mother announced firmly. "At least then I'll know what he's up to and that he's safe."

"Call me if there's any problem. Any problems at all. Wish your father well."

"I will," she said with a smile. "Thanks again." She carried the contented and now sleepy child out the door and Hunter waited until the door shut softly before laughing.

"Corn kernels?" Rina said in amusement. "Is that...usual? I mean is this something that happens around here a lot?"

He laughed, dropping an arm around her shoulder as he guided her toward the front door. "This isn't a cultural thing, Rina. This is a toddler thing. All kids try to stuff something up there noses at least once. If I recall, Cutter stuffed an eraser up his."

Laughing, she let him take her toward the truck. "And what did the good doctor stick up his nose?"

He grinned, and she could have sworn he blushed. "A dime."

"A dime," she repeated, slowing her steps to gape at him. Nudging her along whether she wanted to go or not, he shrugged.

"Hey, I was a practical kid, I was saving for a rainy day."

Laughing, she shook her head. "Now where are we going?"

''For some coffee.'' He sighed, opening the truck door for her, and letting his eyes linger on her slender, curvy legs, bare in her shorts.

He could almost feel his mouth watering. Looking at her, touching her did amazing things to his system. ''I'm going to take you to the Blackwell Café. It's right out of the fifties. I think you'll enjoy it.''

With a sigh, Hunter closed the door, grateful they'd be in a public place with lots of people. Then he wouldn't have to worry about controlling his thoughts or emotions, never mind his hands.

The more time he spent with Rina, the more the yearning grew deeper, stronger until it seemed as if it were simply a part of him. Or rather *she* was.

He had vowed never to let another woman entangle his heart. His body, yes, but not his heart. He glanced at Rina as he drove. But this woman had ensnared not just his body, but his heart as well. A dangerous combination he realized, one he had to get a hold of before it led to disaster.

He knew it was wrong; that there could be nothing between them. He wasn't able to trust a woman, he knew that. Not any woman. Not even Rina. Besides, there were too many things standing between them. They were too different, not just their lives, their history and their culture, but even their location. She lived in Chicago; he in Texas. To say nothing about their differences over Billy's custody.

Intellectually he knew all the reasons why he had to stay away from her, why he couldn't let her touch his body or his heart.

But emotionally, he had a sinking feeling he was losing the battle, and right now, he feared he was sorely in danger of losing the war as well.

The blast of cold air from the air-conditioning hit her full in the face, making Rina sigh in grateful relief as she glanced around.

Hunter was right; the Blackwell Café was right out of the fifties and she fell in love with it immediately. With its turquoise plastic booths and scarred Formica tables, the scent of frying onions, and the raucous country-and-western music that filled the air.

Taking a booth near the back, they ordered drinks, then stared out the large plate glass windows at the traffic meandering by.

After a waitress took their order, pie and coffee for Hunter and a large iced tea for Rina, she sat back, grateful for the coolness of the café.

They'd spent most of the day outdoors, and Rina was exhausted. The intense heat had a tendency to drain her strength.

"Hunter, what is that you wear around your neck?"

Absently, Hunter touched the small brown leather pouch given to him as a child by the Shaman. He'd worn it ever since.

"It's an amulet. The Shaman gave it to me when I was just a small boy."

"Does it have some special significance?" She couldn't remember ever seeing him without it.

"It is said that by wearing it, it will protect from the Spirits of Evil."

"What's in it?"

"Ha-dintin." At her frown, he explained. *"Ha-dintin* is the pollen of tule cattails, believed by The People to protect from the Spirits of Evil," he said as the waitress slid their orders in front of them.

She glanced around the café. The place was dotted with customers here and there, and everyone seemed to know everyone else. Including—no, especially—Hunter.

She smiled at him as he sat sipping coffee, something that made her shake her head.

"What?" he asked, taking another sip of his steaming coffee.

"How can you drink hot coffee when it's so hot out?"

"Seems to me you drank plenty of it this morning."

"Yeah, but that was for survival. Hunter," she said abruptly. "What's wrong?"

He'd stopped listening. He was craning his neck to see around her and out the window. She heard the police siren, then turned to look out the window, following Hunter's and everyone else's gaze.

A police car with its lights flashing and its siren blaring ran aground at the curb as it screeched to a stop.

The car was still rocking when the door flew open. As Colt, who Rina had learned was the town sheriff, got out, Rina felt a shiver race over her.

"Something must be wrong," Hunter said, getting to his feet. "Colt may be crazy, but he's not reckless."

"Hunter," Colt said, opening the door before Hunter got there. "I've been looking for you all morning." He glanced at Rina, flashed her a grin and a wink, then turned his attention back to Hunter, all business now.

Hunter frowned. "What's up, Colt? Why have you been looking for me?"

Colt glanced at Rina, then back at Hunter. "Why don't you buy me a cup of coffee, bro?" His intention was clear. He wanted to speak to Hunter. Alone.

It was hard to feel insulted when Colt flashed her a charming smile as he dropped an affectionate arm around his brother and led him toward the counter.

They spoke in rapid whispers for a moment, before Colt exited the restaurant as quickly as he'd entered.

Slowly, his eyes dark, Hunter returned to the booth.

"What's the matter?" Rina asked nervously.

He sighed as he sat back down, reaching for the check and his wallet at the same time.

"Billy's grandfather has been taken to the hospital."

"I'm so sorry." Remembering how much this man meant to Hunter, she reached out to cover his hand with hers. "Hunter, is he going to be all right?"

"I don't know." Hunter pulled out bills from his

wallet, then let his troubled gaze meet Rina's. "Hallie Lost Souls is with him. Colt said he drove the Wise One to the hospital himself."

Hunter sighed, trying to count out the money and not let his rapid thoughts interfere with the process.

The Wise One was traditional, and did not see the need for or believe in hospitals.

Hunter ached for what he knew would be a painful time for the old man. Worry about the old man's condition only caused more unease.

Rina's eyes suddenly turned wide with worry of her own. "Hunter, if Billy's grandfather's been taken to the hospital, then...where's Billy?" Her heart had begun to hammer in trepidation.

He didn't answer her immediately, carefully counting out the bills again, and then slowly rising to his feet.

He shook his head, before letting his worry-filled gaze meet hers. "He's run away, Rina." Hunter reached for his keys on the table and heaved a long, weary sigh. "Billy's run away."

Chapter Six

"I'm going with you," Rina said, coming out onto the front porch to watch Hunter hurriedly pack the last of his gear in the back of the pickup.

She'd been deathly afraid he planned to leave without her.

Something she wasn't about to allow.

With icy fingers of fear gripping her, she'd sat in the front seat of the truck as Hunter drove straight from the café to the Blackwell ranch.

He hadn't spoken a word to her during the ride, and her own worries were such that she couldn't seem to find her voice.

All she kept thinking of was the fact that Billy had run away.

Fresh worry filled her heart when Hunter had ushered her inside the house, then proceeded to ignore her as he went about packing up his truck.

"I'm going with you," she repeated, coming down the stairs of the sprawling ranch house.

"No, you're not," he said quietly, his mouth grim as he tightened down the rope that held the gear in the flatbed of the truck.

"Yes, I am," Rina retorted just as firmly, determined not to be shunted aside.

He'd been hoping she would merely stay at the ranch with Sadie and wait for him to return from the search. His own worries were laying heavily upon him, and he did not wish to add her to the list.

Billy had been in the canyons with his grandfather, and it was a sure bet he was still there.

Somewhere.

As many times as Billy had been in the canyon, Hunter still doubted the boy could find his way out alone. It could be deep and dangerous even if you knew your way around. If you didn't... The thought terrified him.

Hunter jumped down off the flatbed and let his eyes slowly, deliberately wander over her.

"Rina, be practical. You don't know the canyon, and you're not accustomed to the terrain. It could be dangerous for you, besides, having you with me will merely slow me down."

He didn't want to add that having her with him would only be a distraction right now, and he needed to keep his wits about him if he was going to find Billy. He also didn't want to be worrying about her.

But the truth of the matter was he didn't trust himself in her presence. Searching the canyon would no doubt take all night. He'd have to find a place outdoors to bunk, and the thought of lying beside Rina, under the stars in the dark of night might prove to be more than he could handle right now.

He wasn't so sure that he could keep himself, or his emotions under control now, especially when he was worried about the Shaman and about Billy.

He needed all his faculties about him in order to concentrate on the task before him.

She had disrupted him more than he cared for, more than he'd ever allowed a woman. Disrupted and disturbed him so that she was constantly crowding his thoughts, and his gaze was constantly seeking her out.

There was something far too...primitive humming between them, something elemental and far too dangerous. He was old enough to recognize one part as attraction, and smart enough to know that the emotions that had risen along with it were only complicating things for him.

And his peace.

For all their sakes, especially his own, he had to do this alone.

"Tough." Hands on hips, Rina glared at him. "I'm going with you. Just give me a minute to change."

"The sun will be setting soon." Placing a hand

over his eyes to shield them, Hunter looked toward the sky. "I don't want to waste precious daylight. The canyon can be treacherous at night."

Or anytime for someone who was not experienced, and did not know his way.

Or for someone who did not wish to be alone with a red-haired mischief maker who had the ability to touch him in ways he did not want to be touched.

"I'll hurry." She took a step forward, laying a hand on his arm. Her gaze sought his and the sadness, the worry in his eyes immediately softened her annoyance at his insistence that she remain behind.

"Hunter, I have just as much at stake here as you." She stepped closer, wanting to comfort, to soothe. "Together, we'll find him. I know it." Standing on tiptoe, she brushed her lips gently against his, and felt nerves begin to hum all the way to the tips of her toes.

"I'll be right back," she whispered, praying her knees wouldn't buckle. Rina turned on her heel and fled back into the house, determined to grab what she needed and change quickly.

Hunter stood still, letting the heat of the afternoon seep into him, through him, trying to calm the worry that was making him edgy and find the peace that had been eluding him since the day Rina had arrived.

"Here's some grub for the trip." Sadie plopped a picnic basket stuffed with food that she'd packed into a cooler into the back of his truck, then handed him a long, cool glass of lemonade. "Looks to me like you got your hands full.'' She nodded toward the house and couldn't help but smile. ''She might be little but she's a spirited one, I'll give you that.'' Sadie laughed. ''Reminds me of your mama when she was young. When she and your dad first started courting.''

Hunter sighed, dragging a hand through his hair. ''We're not courting,'' he said with gritted teeth, not wanting anyone to get the wrong impression.

''Uh-huh,'' Sadie said with a twinkle in her eye, watching Hunter's eyes follow Rina's every movement as she raced back out of the house, hugging one of his brother's sweatshirts in her arms. ''Not courting at all,'' Sadie confirmed with a satisfied grin.

He opened his mouth to protest, but his eyes went over Rina and his mouth couldn't seem to work.

She'd changed. Dressed in another one of her mouthwatering T-shirts and a leg-baring pair of shorts, the soft white cotton of her shirt gently caressed the small, gentle curves of her breasts. His mouth went as dry as the dust swirling around him, remembering how she'd tasted, felt.

''Let's get going.''

Abruptly, he turned away from her, walking around the truck, checking his gear one more time, before climbing behind the wheel. He waited for her to get in, not offering to help, not trusting himself to be that near her while his body was aching, and his soul craving.

Rina climbed in, grateful for the blast of air-

PLAY SILHOUETTE'S

LUCKY HEARTS

GAME

AND YOU GET

FREE BOOKS!
A FREE GIFT!
AND MUCH MORE!

TURN THE PAGE AND DEAL YOURSELF IN...

Play **LUCKY HEARTS** for this...

exciting FREE gift!
This surprise mystery gift could be yours free

when you play **LUCKY HEARTS!**
...then continue your lucky streak with a sweetheart of a deal!

1. Play Lucky Hearts as instructed on the opposite page.
2. Send back this card and you'll receive brand-new Silhouette Special Edition® novels. These books have a cover price of $4.50 each in the U.S. and $5.25 each in Canada, but they are yours to keep absolutely free.
3. There's no catch! You're under no obligation to buy anything. We charge nothing—ZERO—for your first shipment. And you don't have to make any minimum number of purchases—not even one!
4. The fact is thousands of readers enjoy receiving books by mail from the Silhouette Reader Service™. They enjoy the convenience of home delivery...they like getting the best new novels at discount prices, BEFORE they're available in stores...and they love their *Heart to Heart* subscriber newsletter featuring author news, horoscopes, recipes, book reviews and much more!
5. We hope that after receiving your free books you'll want to remain a subscriber. But the choice is yours—to continue or cancel, any time at all! So why not take us up on our invitation, with no risk of any kind. You'll be glad you did!

- ◆ **Exciting Silhouette romance novels—FREE!**
- ◆ **Plus an exciting mystery gift—FREE!**

YES!

I have scratched off the silver card. Please send me the 2 FREE books and gift for which I qualify.
I understand I am under no obligation to purchase any books, as explained on the back and on the opposite page.

With a coin, scratch off the silver card and check below to see what we have for you.

SILHOUETTE'S
LUCKY HEARTS GAME

335 SDL CY39

235 SDL CY33
(S-SE-03/00)

| | | | | | | | | | | | | | | | | | |
NAME (PLEASE PRINT CLEARLY)

| | | | | | | | | | | | | | | | | | |
ADDRESS

| | | | | | | | | | | | | | | | | | |
APT.# CITY

| | | | | | | | | | | | | | | | | | |
STATE/PROV. ZIP/POSTAL CODE

Twenty-one gets you 2 free books, and a free mystery gift!

Twenty gets you 2 free books!

Nineteen gets you 1 free book!

Try Again!

Offer limited to one per household and not valid to current Silhouette Special Edition® subscribers. All orders subject to approval.

The Silhouette Reader Service™—Here's how it works:

Accepting your 2 free books and gift places you under no obligation to buy anything. You may keep the books and gift and return the shipping statement marked "cancel." If you do not cancel, about a month later we'll send you 6 additional novels and bill you just $3.80 each in the U.S., or $4.21 each in Canada, plus 25¢ delivery per book and applicable taxes if any.* That's the complete price and — compared to cover prices of $4.50 each in the U.S. and $5.25 each in Canada — it's quite a bargain! You may cancel at any time, but if you choose to continue, every month we'll send you 6 more books, which you may either purchase at the discount price or return to us and cancel your subscription.

*Terms and prices subject to change without notice. Sales tax applicable in N.Y. Canadian residents will be charged applicable provincial taxes and GST.

If offer card is missing write to: Silhouette Reader Service, 3010 Walden Ave., P.O. Box 1867, Buffalo, NY 14240-1867

BUSINESS REPLY MAIL
FIRST-CLASS MAIL   PERMIT NO. 717   BUFFALO, NY

POSTAGE WILL BE PAID BY ADDRESSEE

SILHOUETTE READER SERVICE
3010 WALDEN AVE
PO BOX 1867
BUFFALO NY 14240-9952

NO POSTAGE
NECESSARY
IF MAILED
IN THE
UNITED STATES

conditioning that immediately cooled her skin. She was silent as Hunter started the truck and drove down the long, winding driveway before pulling onto the road.

She glanced around. If she wasn't mistaken, they were heading in the opposite direction from where the canyon was.

"Hunter?" she asked. "Is this the way to the canyon?"

"No."

"No?" She turned toward him, wondering why he was being so taciturn. "No," she repeated again with a sigh. Folding her hands in her lap, she took a deep breath, praying for patience. "Okay, if this is not the way to the canyon, then it's on the way to...where?"

"The hospital." He spared her a glance. "I need to speak to the Shaman. The canyon is large and he was the last one to see Billy. They had probably traveled from his hogan to one of the many streams to fish. I need to find out exactly where they were so I'll know where to begin the search, otherwise we could be searching in vain for days."

"Days?" Rina swallowed hard and laced her fingers together as fear and nerves mingled. "I can't imagine Billy being all alone out there...for days."

The panic came then, almost overwhelming her. She'd been through so much, she wasn't certain she could handle any more. But she realized she didn't have much choice.

With a sigh, Hunter pressed harder on the accelerator, letting his own worries get to him. He glanced at Rina, realizing she was just as concerned.

"We'll find him," he assured her, covering her hand with his. When she turned her palm up and gripped his hand, they laced their fingers together and held on.

"Do you know how the Shaman is?"

"Colt said he was in pretty bad shape when they brought him in. I've suspected he's had a heart condition for a while." He glanced in the rearview mirror. "The Shaman is traditional. He will not find it a comfort to be in a hospital with people—strangers fussing around him."

"But he's sick," she protested.

"Yes, Rina, he is sick. You and I know that, but to the Shaman, illness is just another part of life, part of the wondrous cycle. He believes that his own powers will heal him if that's what is destined."

"And if it's not?" she asked.

Hunter sighed again. "Then Billy will suffer another loss," he said quietly, glancing out the window.

And, he thought sadly, so would he.

Blackwell Community Hospital was located right on the outskirts of town. A small, low-slung cement building with several buildings jutting off on each side, Hunter made his way through the hospital as if he belonged there, and then Rina realized with a start, he did.

He led her up to the second floor, via the steps,

not wanting to take the time to wait for the elevators, and down a long, narrow hallway that smelled of antiseptic and stale coffee. He went to the nurses' station to speak with one of the nurses.

Rina huddled nearby, not wanting to appear nosy. She sighed as a stab of jealousy hit her and she watched the nurse bat her eyelashes at Hunter in the same manner as the young girl at the airport had done. Obviously, more than one woman felt the need to flirt whenever Hunter was around.

She knew the feeling. Vividly.

Sighing, Rina scooped her tangled hair off her face as she watched Hunter, unable to take her eyes away from him.

Hunter examined a chart, then said something to the nurse, before turning on his heel and heading down the hall, pausing to pull Rina to her feet and along down the hallway with him.

He stopped outside of a room, then turned to her. "Rina?"

Her gaze searched his. She could read nothing in his eyes. "What?" she asked, dragging a hand through her hair. She wasn't certain she could bear the look of sadness on his face. He looked…lost. As if he had the weight of the world on his shoulders.

She understood the feeling of helplessness, knowing someone you loved was ill, and there was little you could do.

"Hunter if you've got something to say, please say it. I don't have any special powers, so I can't read your mind."

Her vain attempt at humor made him smile. Gently, he laid his hands on her shoulders, torn between his loyalty to the Shaman, and this sudden, urgent need he had to protect her, from what, he wasn't certain.

And then he realized the only thing she needed protection from was...him.

"Hunter?" His touch immediately sent off warning bells. Her knees grew rubbery and her pulse kicked into high gear, but it was the look on his face, so grave, so serious that had her trembling. "What is it?"

"It is important not to...disturb the Shaman any more than necessary."

His words immediately annoyed her and she placed her hands on her hips, glaring up at him. "Geez, Hunter, you've ruined my plans. I was going to go screeching and cartwheeling into his room."

This time he did laugh, and she felt some of the tension leave her. Hunter shook his head. "I'm sorry, I didn't mean to seem...insensitive, it's just—"

She laid a hand on his chest, then tipped her head back to look at him. "It's all right, I understand. You're upset—"

Their eyes met and held and some deep, powerful, frightening emotion shimmered between them.

Rina swallowed hard, not certain why the man had such an impact on her, only knowing that looking at him, touching him, filled her heart with a joy she'd never experienced before.

Hunter covered her hand with his, savoring the warmth of her touch, the silkiness of her skin. He wanted to pull her to him, to hold her, to cradle her to him, to lose himself in her. To find some relief from this aching yearning that was growing stronger and more powerful with each passing day.

An aching that filled his body as well as his empty soul.

His gaze dropped to her lips, and he remembered their taste, their softness, and remembered too that he craved more, craved the taste of her the way a dying man craved absolution.

How he wanted her.

He understood that.

What frightened him was that he was beginning to worry that he *needed* her.

The former he could handle.

The latter he couldn't allow. Not now. Not ever.

"Rina." He swallowed hard, then continued. "I want to go in to see the Shaman myself. I want to check his condition, and assure him that I will find Billy and bring him home safely."

"*We* will find Billy," she corrected.

"Will you wait for me out here?" His gaze searched hers and she sighed.

"Yes, I'll wait out here." Now she understood. He feared her mere presence would disturb the Shaman. She tried not to let it bother her, tried not to care what he thought of her.

"I have no desire to disturb him, Hunter." There was an echo of sadness in her voice, in her heart.

No one had ever quite treated her like she was an…unfit person before, and she found that it hurt. "Nor do I have any intention of bringing up the custody issue or why I'm really here while the man is so ill." She blinked back tears. "I'm not heartless, you know."

"I'm sorry." Feeling miserable, he gathered her close, wanting to comfort her, but needing a little comfort himself. "I didn't mean to insult or hurt you."

She wrapped her arms around his slender waist and sighed, snuggling closer.

"Will you be all right by yourself?" he asked.

She nodded, lifting her head to look at him.

"Good." Unable to resist, he lowered his head and gently covered her lips with his own.

She immediately felt the world tilt crazily. His kiss this time was gentle, coaxing, comforting. It felt as natural and normal as her own skin.

Moaning softly, she wound her arms tighter around him, wishing they weren't standing in the middle of a public place with people milling and rushing about.

Hunter drew back, tenderly brushing the curls from her face, wondering, worrying about what this woman was doing to him. "Have a seat. I'll be right back."

Nodding, Rina found a lone chair against the wall and sat. After their early-morning trek to Mary's, the emergency with Joey Whitecloud, and now this nonsense with Billy, her nerves were ragged and fatigue was setting in. She was grateful to have a few moments to herself, to think about all that had happened.

With a tired sigh, Rina closed her eyes, letting the fatigue steal over her.

Always honest, especially with herself, she realized in spite of her own resolves, Hunter had the ability, on more than one level, to hurt her. Not just because of Billy, which was more than enough reason not to trust him, but because of her own feelings, feelings she could no longer deny, or control.

It was hopeless, she realized. Hopeless because of the situation with Billy. She knew he didn't trust what was between them; wouldn't speak of it or acknowledge it. What she didn't know was why.

She had a feeling it wasn't simply the fact that he didn't believe she could or should have custody of Billy. No, she knew it was something more. Much more.

He hadn't talked about his past, or his past experiences with women, other than with his birth mother. Rina frowned, wondering if perhaps there was something else in Hunter's past, some experience with a woman that had him holding himself back from her.

"Rina?" He touched her shoulder, startling her. Her eyes flew open and she jumped to her feet, stifling a yawn, embarrassed at being caught napping.

"What?" She rubbed her eyes, trying to clear her blurred vision.

"The Shaman would like to see you." His words made her stiffen.

"Me?" She pushed a tangle of hair off her face, trying not to be alarmed as an older, Native American man dressed in traditional clothing slipped out of the Shaman's room.

Curiosity made her wonder who he was, but not enough to ask.

"Why?" she asked so skeptically, Hunter chuckled, taking her hand and pulling her toward the Shaman's room before she could protest. "Why does the Shaman want to see me?"

"Because," was all he said, as he pushed her toward the room.

"Well, geez, that explains everything. Did he tell you where they were?"

"Yes. He and Billy were fishing in a stream not far from the Shaman's summer hogan. I know the area well. The Shaman and I spent many moons fishing there when I was a child." He came to a sudden stop right in front of the open hospital door and she almost bumped into him. "Remember what I said," he cautioned, as he gave her a nudge toward the single bed in the room. "Let's not upset him. He's had a massive heart attack."

Swallowing hard, Rina nodded, pushing her hair off her face again, wondering why she was so blasted nervous.

The man in the bed looked so small and so still. His hair was steel gray, parted down the middle and arranged neatly in two long braids that rested on his frail shoulders.

His face was tanned and weathered by life and the sun, creasing deep lines into the skin.

The Shaman was hooked up to machines that beeped and bleated, while an IV tube ran liquid from a bag on a pole, into his arm.

His eyes were closed, but then slowly, very slowly they opened and looked at her for a long, long moment.

She tried not to fidget.

His eyes were a deep, pale blue, clouded a bit by what she guessed were the beginnings of cataracts.

He lifted a wrinkled hand and motioned her closer. She glanced at Hunter over her shoulder, waiting for his nod of approval before moving closer to the bed.

The Shaman just kept staring at her, and then his gaze shifted to Hunter and he said something in his native tongue.

Rina glanced back at Hunter, who now stood directly behind her, so close she could feel the warmth of his body radiating against hers. If she leaned back just a bit, they would be touching.

"What did he say?" she whispered.

Hunter tried not to smile, but couldn't quite manage it. "He said you look like you need a good meal."

Not in the least bit insulted, Rina smiled at the old man's observation as he said something else to Hunter.

"He said it is good that you've come to show that Billy has family. It is a sign of pride for a young boy to have family."

"Does he know why I'm here?" she whispered, and Hunter gave a perceptible shake of his head.

"No." Hunter's gaze met hers, and he didn't say a word but she could almost hear what he was thinking.

And you're not going to tell him.

Slowly, the old man reached for her hand. His grip was weak, but his skin was warm as his eyes met hers.

His voice was thin, raspy and weak, as he whispered something that Hunter had to bend to hear.

"I will tell her."

Hunter turned to her, and she saw something in his gaze, something warm and gentle that almost made her toes curl.

"He said that the love you have for your nephew is spoken in your eyes. He said he shares that love. And that once he is better and Billy has returned from his wayward journey, you two will speak of the boy's future."

Rina's heart fluttered with joy, and her gaze shifted to the Shaman, and in spite of his weakness, he squeezed her hand and managed a slow smile before letting his eyes close, his hand still clutching hers.

"Rest, Grandfather," Hunter said softly, laying a hand on the old man's head, then bending to kiss his forehead. "We will find him. Do not worry."

Chapter Seven

Dusk was coming quickly and the shadows of the sun were long and deep as Hunter and Rina drove toward the canyon.

They left the main road, and were now bumping along a dusty makeshift piece of land which wasn't quite a road, but couldn't actually qualify as a gully.

"Where are we?" she finally asked, glancing out the window and trying not to feel trepidation.

They seemed to have left civilization behind and she tried to remember how wide and large the reservation was, but it still felt as if they were driving off the end of the world. Perhaps because Hunter had not brought her this way before.

"On the reservation."

"I know, but..." She glanced around again.

"But...but I don't see any people." It was unusual. Almost everywhere Hunter had taken her, the reservation had been teeming with people.

He smiled. "That's because we're on what's considered the back side of the canyon. Not many people live on this side. It's almost uninhabitable. This is still considered sacred, ancient land, still pure, still mainly used as a hunting and fishing area."

He glanced at her, but only for a moment since the terrain was so rough he had to pay attention to the road.

"Most of the homesteads are on the other side," he explained, "but this road is quicker to the canyon, although it's not used very often because it's so desolate."

"I believe the word is *unpaved*," she said with a frown, as he hit a particularly hard bump that had her nearly hitting her head on the top of the truck.

A bird soared, then screamed overhead, and Rina felt a shiver, rubbing her hands up and down her chilled arms.

Automatically, Hunter turned down the air-conditioning. The air had turned a bit cooler, and the lower and deeper they went into the canyon, the cooler and darker it would become.

"Are you frightened?" he asked, glancing at her.

"No," she said a bit hesitantly. "Not frightened about going into the canyon." She smiled. "Besides, I'm never frightened when I'm with you."

He wouldn't feel pleased or proud. He simply

wouldn't allow it, but still his chest expanded as he reached for her hand.

"But I am frightened about finding Billy," Rina continued. She glanced out the window, vividly aware now that the barren land seemed to go on forever. "How are we ever going to find him out here?" She shook her head, not convinced they could find anything or anyone in this vast expanse of space. "I don't think I've ever been anywhere where I didn't see...some people."

"This is a good place to come when one needs to find peace. To become one with the universe."

"Yes, I can see that," Rina said with a frown. "It is...peaceful, I suppose." She watched the makeshift road curve and then dip suddenly, tilting almost straight down. "Having no people around would have a tendency to make you feel like you're one with the universe."

Hunter pumped on the brakes as the truck pitched forward, nose down, making her feel like she had climbed aboard a roller coaster. Her empty stomach dipped, then pitched, and she groaned softly.

"Are you all right?" he asked, glancing at her quickly and trying to steer the truck at the same time.

She nodded, not trusting herself to speak. "How...how much farther?" she asked, pressing a hand against her protesting tummy.

"In the truck?" Hunter glanced in his rearview mirror. "Perhaps another half mile or so."

"And then?" She was absolutely positive she

wasn't going to like whatever came after the "in the truck" part.

"Then we'll walk the rest of the way down."

"Walk." She swallowed. "We're going to walk?" Her voice cracked on the last word, remembering all the time she'd already spent walking over the many acres of reservation.

He smiled, trying not to be amused at the look on her face. "Yes, walk," he confirmed, glancing at her sturdy tennis shoes. "You do remember how to do that, don't you?" He was hoping his teasing might ease some of the tension in her face.

"I wish I didn't," she admitted, too afraid to look down to see if her feet were still there, and if more importantly, they were in any condition to be doing any more walking today.

The deeper they drove into the canyon, the more alone and desolate she felt, perhaps because it was so...silent.

"I can't imagine Billy being out here—down here," she corrected, trying not to shiver again, "all alone. He has to be terrified."

"Only things we're not used to terrify us, Rina," Hunter said gently. "The unknown is always a bit frightening, but you have to remember, Billy was raised on this land, on the reservation, and he's been coming down into the canyon with his grandfather since he was just a little boy. This is home to him, just like his own private backyard. I can't imagine that being here would frighten him."

She tried to be reassured by his words, but found

she wasn't. "It's an awfully big backyard for a four-teen-year-old boy."

The ground leveled, then flattened, and abruptly Hunter pulled the truck to the side where a large piece of flat, gravel land seemed to spring out of nowhere. He turned off the ignition, then rolled up the window.

"Are you ready?"

She swallowed again. "This is the 'after the truck' part, isn't it?" she asked nervously, and he nodded, trying not to smile.

She was trying to be brave, but failing miserably.

"Now, we'll have to walk the rest of the way down. The road's too steep and curvy to drive and it's no longer paved. Plus, there are too many ridges and bluffs we have to check to do it by car."

He threw open the door and climbed out, going around the back to unload all his gear.

He had no idea how long it would take to find Billy, but he'd packed enough for them to camp in the canyon overnight if it became necessary.

Glancing at the setting sun, he realized it probably would be necessary.

His gaze shifted to Rina and he realized he wasn't certain he could handle spending the night alone with her.

He hoped they'd find Billy soon.

"Can I carry something?" she asked as she watched him strap on a backpack filled with his camping gear and what he'd deemed necessary supplies, not that he deemed it necessary to inform her what those supplies were.

He'd also slipped his portable cell phone into the backpack before he'd climbed out of the car.

She noticed, then, that he'd also strapped a sheathed knife to his leather belt when she apparently wasn't looking.

"What on earth is that?" She pointed, eyes wide.

He glanced down. "It's a hunting knife."

"A hunting knife," she repeated, giving him another arch look that had him almost chuckling. She rocked back on her heels, biting the inside of her cheek. "Planning to do some operating, Doctor?"

This time he did chuckle. "Not unless you want to volunteer as a patient."

She shook her head. "Can't. I faint at the sight of blood."

"So do I."

It took her a moment to realize he was teasing, and that he was deliberately trying to ease some of her fears, and it only endeared him to her.

"Why are you wearing a knife?" A sudden thought had her casting a quick glance around, as she scooted closer to him. "Are there—" her gaze darted about again "—animals out here?" She said the word *animals,* the same way anyone else might would have said *aliens.*

For a city girl, the mere thought of animals, not in cages or in the zoo, but out in the open, close enough to see or perhaps touch, was enough to send her scurrying back into the truck.

She tried to peer over the ridge they were on, but couldn't see too much since they apparently were on some type of flat landing.

She wasn't certain she wanted to get near the edge. Or look down.

"There are some animals," he said, as he picked up Sadie's packed picnic basket and handed it to her. "But they won't bother you if you don't bother them."

"I can do that," she assured him with a furious nod of her head. "I can definitely not be bothersome." When she caught his smile, she glowered at him. "Well, I can certainly try," she amended stiffly, not amused by his apparent amusement.

"Can you carry that?" he asked as she slung the picnic basket over her arm, wondering if it was too heavy for her slight, slender body.

"As long as I can use it as a weapon if any creepy-crawlers come near me," Rina replied on a frustrated breath.

"Stay close to me," Hunter ordered, as he stepped off the flattened ground and onto the unpaved, rocky area.

"As if I planned on going off on a solitary excursion," she muttered, following close behind him, grabbing on to his belt merely for the security of it. "Where are we headed?"

Walking behind him, she couldn't help but admire his male...form. With a sigh, she realized she'd never quite appreciated the male form before. At least not one like Hunter's.

"Toward a spring near the Shaman's summer hogan. It's near the mouth of the canyon. The Shaman and Billy were fishing there this morning, before Billy took off. It is their special place."

The land continued to spiral downward, but Hunter walked slowly, mindful of his footfalls, acutely aware that Rina was right behind him and a novice at this. Not to mention she was terrified of heights.

"Hunter, did the Shaman tell you what happened? Why Billy ran away?" she asked.

"Billy was supposed to be packing the fish in dry leaves. He was gone too long and his grandfather went to look for him. That's when the Shaman realized that Billy was gone."

Inhaling slowly, Hunter held the air in for a long moment, enjoying the peace and quiet that surrounded him and the warm, fresh air, unpolluted by humans or anything else.

This was nature at its most beautiful, and he felt some of his peace return.

Until he glanced back at Rina.

She was winded, he could see. Her cheeks were flushed a bit pink from exertion, and he knew her legs were probably getting tired.

He reached out and relieved her of the picnic basket, slinging it over his own arm to ease her burden a bit.

"The Shaman set out to look for Billy, and became ill after several hours of searching."

"How did your brother Colt find him?" Rina

asked with a frown, pausing to dig a pebble out of her tennis shoe and rest for a moment. She glanced over the edge of the ridge. The canyon seemed to drop.

Way down.

Her stomach dropped again.

"Oh, my word," she exclaimed, eyes wide, one shoe on, one shoe off as she hobbled closer to the edge to look below.

Down below—way, way below—she could see the sandy ground, in different, varying shades that shifted from brown to gray. It was beautiful in its absolute starkness.

"Don't get so close." Instinctively, Hunter placed an arm protectively around her shoulders, pulling her back a bit. His mere touch reminded her that they were all alone in this vast expanse of land, and she was suddenly vividly aware, too, of the rapid beating of her heart.

He was standing right next to her, close enough so that she could feel the warmth of his body heat radiating against her. Close enough that their bodies were touching, close enough to make her wonder what on earth was happening to her.

Emotions battered her. Fear, longing, desire. And panic. If her legs weren't weak before, they were now.

"Colt didn't find the Shaman," Hunter said, acutely aware that having his arm protectively around her smaller, slender frame seemed the most natural thing in he world. She fit as if she had been made for him. But he'd known that since the night he'd first felt the need to hold her in his arms.

Through her thin, cotton shirt, he could feel the warm softness of her skin, the fragile slenderness of her shoulder. Hunter swallowed hard, trying not to think of the creamy skin under the T-shirt, or how she'd feel beneath him.

"Hallie Lost Souls is always with the Shaman," he said, forcing himself to keep his mind on his words, and not on the feelings swamping him. "After they'd been searching for a while, he realized the Wise One was not well, and went for help. Since Colt's the sheriff, he called him."

She glanced up at him, and was caught short by his closeness, wishing she knew what to do with her hands.

He was so close, she simply wanted to touch him, to lay a gentle hand across the planes and angles of his beautiful face, to smooth a finger over his brow, his eyes, to touch her lips to his, to drink from him until she was sated, satisfied.

She swallowed hard, then as if mesmerized, lifted a hand to his cheek. Hunter merely stared at her, his eyes widening a bit.

"H-Hallie Lost Souls. Is—is he the gentleman who was slipping out the door of the Shaman's hospital room as we were going in?" Her voice was threadier than she would have liked, and not from the climb.

Hunter slid his hand to her waist, drawing her closer until she was tilting her head up to look at him, their mouths only inches apart. He felt his chest expand with the effort to take a deep breath. "To call Hallie Lost Souls a gentleman would be to tickle his funny bone," he whispered softly. He bent his head, rubbing his lips over hers in a teasing seductive motion that had her gasping for breath and reaching for him with a moan.

She pulled him closer, letting his mouth take her deeper into the well of passion. She clung, holding on to him, arching against him, wanting to quench the need and desire in her body, in her heart that had been simmering and brewing from the moment she'd laid eyes on him.

Hunter shifted, sliding his hands to her waist, then lower, to pull her closer against his aching hardness, wanting to quench the raw, raging hunger that had been released the moment he'd laid eyes on her.

Emotions raw and deep swamped him. He couldn't ever remember wanting—needing—anything this much before.

It wasn't just his body that ached to be filled, but his heart, his soul, the places that he'd never let anyone touch. Or see.

Except his family.

He'd closed off his emotions when it came to women years before, knowing it would only bring pain and desolation, but now, holding Rina, wanting her, needing her with his body and soul, suddenly terrified him.

He drew back with the warning clanging in his mind, and desire swirling through his body.

With his eyes still on hers, he looked at her, stroked the gentle swell of her cheek, but kept her close, their bodies still touching, still aroused.

"I...I..." He swallowed, swore softly under his breath, feeling like a sixteen-year-old having a testosterone tantrum. He wanted to yank her close, to peel her clothes off, to peel away the protective layers he'd built around himself, to lose himself in her, body and soul, to tell her what was building, growing inside of him for her.

The feelings and the needs were so powerful they frightened him, for he knew they jeopardized all that he had worked so hard for, for so many years: his inner peace, his solitude, the life he'd built.

A life that until this moment he hadn't realized was empty and lonely.

So lonely.

He believed a man was meant to have a mate. He'd had no finer example than his parents Emma and Justin. But he didn't know if he could ever trust himself—trust a woman—enough to give up the barrier of protection he'd built against the pain and betrayal loving a woman could bring.

He'd never thought he'd have to worry about it.

Until Rina.

She'd slipped past all the emotional barriers he'd built with her gentle, caring ways and her loving nature.

"Hunter." Licking her still-swollen lips, she lifted a hand to his cheek. Her gaze sought his and held. "Tell me, what is it?"

He swallowed again, not trusting himself to speak. All that was in his heart swelled, and threatened to bloom into something he wasn't certain he was ready to accept or handle.

Not yet.

Maybe not ever.

He sighed, dropping his hand from her waist, breaking the contact so that he could think, speak.

"We'd better get going." He glanced toward the horizon. "It will be dark soon."

Frowning, Rina looked at him for a long moment before nodding. She knew he'd wanted to say something about what was happening between them, but something was holding him back from opening his mouth, his heart.

With a sigh, she dragged her hair back and nodded, deciding not to push it. For the moment.

"Okay." She glanced up at him, confused and a bit hurt by his constant withdrawal from her. With her blood still thrumming through her veins, she needed a few minutes to get her bearings. "Got anything to drink in that backpack?"

He smiled, thankful the tension was dissipating. "I think we can dig something up." Grateful for the distraction, Hunter set the picnic basket down before shrugging off his backpack.

Rina asked, "Hunter, tell me about Hallie Lost Souls. Why did you say calling him a gentleman would be to tickle his funny bone?" She accepted the can of lemonade he'd dug out of the basket, and popped the top, drinking greedily, not realizing how thirsty she was.

After opening a can for himself, and taking a long, refreshing sip, Hunter considered her question. "Hallie Lost Souls is an embarrassment to The People. But the Shaman has a loyalty and affection for him that goes deeper, beyond embarrassment."

"Why is Hallie an embarrassment to The People?" she asked with a frown. It was clear that Hunter was embarrassed, and it surprised her for she didn't understand it.

He took his time answering her. "It's really difficult to shatter stereotypes."

"That's true," she said slowly. "But what does that have to do with Hallie Lost Souls?"

"Hallie Lost Souls is what The People consider a lost soul. Thus his name. He drinks too much," he finally concluded in a tone that said more than his words.

"I see." She rocked back on her heels, balancing her lemonade can on her hip. "So the man drinks too much. Is that why he's considered lost, and an embarrassment?" She shook her head. "My father drank too much. In fact, Hunter, he was what I'd call a falling-down hopeless drunk. Worse, he was a mean drunk." She pushed back the anger and the resentment that she'd carried with her from her childhood, not understanding her father now, years after his death, any more than she had when he was alive. She took a step closer to him.

"That's how my parents were killed. My father

insisting on driving home after he'd been drinking at a party." She glanced away, scuffing the toe of her sneakers along the dry, dusty ground, embarrassed and not quite certain why. "He hit another car head-on. His drinking killed both him and my mother." The bitterness was still there, she realized with some surprise. She thought after all these years it would have faded.

"Rina, I'm sorry." Ignoring his own internal warnings about keeping his distance, Hunter pulled her close, resting his chin on the top of her head. "You must have been devastated."

She sighed, enjoying his warmth and comfort, laying a hand to his heart. His touch seemed to soothe some of the anger she'd carried. "I wasn't just devastated. I was barely seventeen. I never had a chance to ease into adulthood. Because of my father's carelessness, I was rudely yanked from being a carefree teenager into a responsible adult whether I was ready for it or not."

He heard her weary sigh, and rubbed a hand up and down her slender back.

She looked up at him. "Just because Hallie is Native American and drinks too much doesn't mean that all Native Americans drink too much, any more than it means that because my father was Irish, and drank too much that all Irishmen drink too much."

"No," he said slowly. "But you have to understand. Historically, Native American men have had to fight the stereotype that if you give us a little 'firewater' we're dangerous."

She laughed at the bitterness in his voice, surprising him. "Hunter, give anyone a little 'firewater,'" she repeated his word with an arch look, "or any other kind of potent liquor, and we're all dangerous. It doesn't have anything to do with culture or race, but more to do with common sense."

He looked at her for a long moment, making her pulse thud again. "You're an unusual woman," he said softly, smiling down at her and realizing she had a point.

"Well, there is that," she said with that sassy smile he'd come to crave.

His gaze drifted over her, drinking in the sight of her.

Her red hair was a curling mass, glinting from the sun, and once again, he couldn't resist touching it, touching her.

From the moment he'd met her, he'd been fighting his own urges, his own impulses, his own fierce yearnings, dueling against his natural tendencies in order to protect his emotions.

The impulse, the yearning was suddenly too strong, too powerful.

He had to touch her.

Just once more, he promised himself.

He reached out and trailed his thumb across her cheek, her lower lip, making her eyes widen with delight, with desire.

He'd never met a woman who was so responsive to him, his touch. He'd had women before Meagan and after her, both as friends and as lovers, but none had ever responded or reacted with the same quick-silver passion as Rina. It delighted and aroused him as never before.

He trailed his finger over her skin. It was warmed from the sun, and as soft as silk, making his fingers itch to touch her in other places.

He heard the clanging then again, as if coming from a long, long distance. It reminded him of the sounds of distant warriors from the stories the Sha-man and other elders of the tribe had told when he was a boy.

He was suddenly reminded that there was more at stake here than his own feelings and desires.

So much more.

His people, his tribe, as well as the Shaman were depending on him; they had all trusted him and he couldn't—wouldn't—let them down.

"Sorry," he said with a smile, showing her his thumb. "You had some dirt on your cheek."

Feeling foolish, Rina nodded and looked away.

"We'd better get going." Still shaken, Hunter glanced at the sun, which would soon be completely buried in the horizon, and darkness, deep and echo-ing, would descend. He'd been in the canyon many times during the night, and knew how peaceful, how silent, how lonely it could be.

It would also be breathtakingly beautiful.

"I'd like to get as close to the Shaman's hogan and the stream as we can tonight. I have a feeling once it starts getting dark, Billy will head back there."

He took her empty can, and placed it, along with his own can in the empty plastic bag Sadie had packed in the picnic basket. He would dispose of it properly once they were off the reservation. "Are you ready?"

She nodded.

"Let's go then." He shrugged back into his backpack, and picked up the picnic basket, then extended his hand toward her. "The road gets very rocky from here on out. I want you to stay close, and hold on to me."

Rina took his hand, trying to ignore the jolt to her heart and her pulse the moment their bodies touched, and let him lead the way.

She heard the water before she saw it. Winded, and nearly weak with exhaustion, Rina glanced up and realized with a great deal of awe that they'd climbed down nearly the entire length of the canyon.

The ground was now finally, blissfully nearly flat and level.

She wanted to fall to her knees and weep with relief.

She glanced around, trying not to be dazzled by the natural beauty that surrounded her.

The air was clear, unpolluted, and so still it seemed as if they were stranded somewhere near the end of the world.

The colors that surrounded her in all their glory were brilliant and rich and almost blinding. The ground was a mix of sand and clay, blending together into a kaleidoscope of beauty that was soft and spongy under her feet.

The silence was almost deafening. Except for the soft sound of the flowing water and the occasional sound of a bird or an animal, there was a deep, natural silence.

The sun was very low in the horizon, casting deep amber and gray shadows across everything. Because they were so deep in the canyon, it was actually pleasantly cool, she noted with relief.

"My God, it's beautiful," Rina said on a deeply expelled breath, as they rounded a bend in the unpaved land and the flowing, clear stream came into view.

In the distance she could see several roofs of what she presumed were huts or houses.

"It is nature at her best," Hunter said softly, bending down to check the ground.

"What are you doing?" She bent as well, not knowing what he was looking at.

"Checking for footprints." He frowned, running his hand over the soft ground. "Billy has been here." He pointed to an impression in the sandy clay. "See the indentation of the land?" He glanced over at her and smiled at her frown.

"You can tell Billy's been here from that?" she asked, still not seeing what he was looking at except a clump of muddy-looking red clay and sand.

"Yes." Hunter frowned, then glanced into the distance. "Billy's been here. More than once if these impressions are to be believed, and not more than four or five hours ago. Which means that he's staying close to what he knows.'' Hunter pointed. ''His grandfather's hogan is just off that way a bit, less than a mile.''

She almost smiled at his description of ''off that way a bit,'' followed by less than a mile. Obviously his definition of *a bit,* and hers, like their ideas of *soon* were clearly different.

''Billy probably realized he wouldn't be able to get out of the canyon from this side. He probably headed toward the other end, toward civilization, and cars.''

''The other end?'' Rina looked at him. ''What's at the other end?'' One brow rose. ''And I think I need more of an explanation about Billy and cars.'' She rolled her eyes as she thought about it. ''Then again, maybe I don't want to know.

Hunter smiled. ''There are two ways into the floor of the canyon. The other side, the side Colt and the search party have taken, is accessible by vehicles. This side is not.''

''You mean we could have driven down here?'' She wasn't going to be annoyed, she told herself. Even though she had leg cramps, heel blisters, and an acute case of height fright, she wasn't going to get annoyed.

He smiled. ''Yes. How do you think the Shaman gets down here? He can no longer walk down, so he has no choice but to use a vehicle.''

''You mean we could have driven down here?''

she asked again, wondering if he enjoyed torturing her.

"Yes," Hunter said patiently, trying not to smile at the obvious dismay on her face. "But then we would have run the risk of not knowing whether Billy had taken this way out. This way both entrances and exits are covered. Colt is on the other side. We're here."

Hunter ran his finger over the ground again.

"My guess is Billy thought about getting out of the canyon from this side, probably even tried it, then thought better of it. It's been a long time since I've brought him down this way, and he probably doesn't remember exactly how to get back up." Hunter turned and glanced up at the canyon, shielding his eyes from the now setting, but still intense sun. "There are many twists and turns, as you know," he added with a smile. "It is easy to get lost, and this is not a place anyone wants to get lost. If he goes out the other side, there is always a chance that he can hitch a ride with someone. Or steal a car," he said with that mischievous smile.

"Steal a what!" She exclaimed, certain she'd heard him wrong.

Hunter laughed. "No, you didn't hear me wrong," he said as if reading her mind. "Billy's at the age where cars are his latest, greatest passion. He'd been driving his father and grandfather nuts to teach him to drive."

"He's not old enough to drive," Rina announced, as if this was news to Hunter.

"I know that, and you know that, but apparently Billy wasn't quite convinced." With a sigh, he dropped his gear and the backpack to the ground, rubbing his aching shoulder. "About three months ago, Hallie Lost Souls found out Billy had been sneaking out during the night to take his grandfather's car for joyrides."

"His grandfather drives?" She couldn't possibly imagine the Shaman driving a car. Or her nephew *stealing* it. No, she wouldn't think of it as stealing. Merely borrowing.

"No, the Shaman doesn't drive." He held up his hand before she could ask. "It was given to him as a gift from a grateful member of the tribe. To refuse a gift would be an insult, something the Shaman would never do. So he had Hallie Lost Souls park it behind his hogan, and it's remained there ever since."

"Exactly when did the Shaman get this car?"

Hunter grinned. "Fifteen years ago. But Hallie faithfully, meticulously takes care of the vehicle as a sign of respect to the gift-giver. Washing it, changing the oil, filling it up with gas, starting it every morning." He shrugged. "Apparently Billy didn't think his grandfather would ever notice."

"So how did he?"

"He didn't," Hunter admitted, realizing by the look that crossed Rina's face that perhaps he had just given her more ammunition in her case that the Shaman could not care for Billy properly. "It was Hallie who noticed the car had been driven." He grinned. ''Billy's smart, but not that smart. He forgot to put gas in the car, and Hallie knew no one else had access to the keys.''

''That little brat,'' Rina said with affection, and just a bit of admiration. ''Although I don't condone his driving or stealing, you have to admit it was pretty ingenious of Billy.''

''Among other things,'' Hunter agreed.

''So, you think Billy's going to try to get out of the canyon from the other side?''

''Probably. The entrance into the canyon from the other side is not nearly as treacherous, and it's a good bet that on any given day someone from the reservation will be driving down, even if its just the tribal police checking for poachers.''

''Poachers?'' she asked in surprise. ''You can't be serious?''

''Absolutely serious,'' he confirmed. ''This land is considered sacred to us. It is a place of peace and harmony, a place of The People, and yet others don't understand the importance or significance of it, and tend to think this land is…a picnic ground open to all for whatever their purpose.'' His voice had taken on an edge. ''Or in the case of teenagers, a perfect lover's lane, or somewhere to hang out and drink.'' Hunter sighed. ''And then of course, there are the adults who like to use our streams for sport fishing. These waters and streams that run through the canyon are totally unpolluted. Every living thing is sacred to us, a part of the universe, a part of the Nature Spirit. We do not kill for sport, only to survive, to feed our families, to take care of our own. As we have for hundreds of years.''

''Family is very important to The People, isn't it?'' she asked quietly, more impressed with the man the more she learned about him.

Hunter smiled. ''Family is the essence of our being.''

''Then why is it, Hunter, that you don't have a family of your own?''

''But I do have family,'' he corrected, standing up, and taking the time to smooth down his jeans so he wouldn't have to look at her. ''Actually two. Emma and Justin Blackwell, my brothers and Sadie. And then there is my tribal family. The Shaman, Billy.''

''I didn't mean a family like a mother, father and brothers. I meant a family like a wife and children of your own.''

He took his time answering, choosing his words carefully. ''I told you it was because I've been too busy with my career, with med school and the usual excuses, but it was not quite the truth. At least not all of it.'' He didn't know if he was ready to continue, to tell her about Meagan or his past experiences with women. Not because it still hurt, it didn't; but simply because it was a shame to him, even now after all these years, that he could have been so naive, so foolish. ''I was engaged,'' he admitted. ''It was a long time ago, when I was in med school.''

"What happened?" she asked softly, sensing she was the one treading on sacred ground now.

His head lifted, his eyes glittered, and for a flash of a moment she saw pain, real, raw, anguished. It nearly tore her heart apart.

"She left me at the altar."

"She was an idiot," Rina snapped with some heat. "It was her loss, Hunter."

"No, it was my gain, Rina." He looked at her long and steady for a moment. "She was from a wealthy family back East. Her father was appalled at the thought of his daughter marrying me." He glanced away. "A half-breed." He laughed, but the sound held no mirth, only a trace of bitterness. "I mean, what would the neighbors think? And the people at the country clubs? The golf clubs." He sighed, wondering why he was even talking about this. "So he offered her the moon and the stars as well as a trip around the world and a villa in France if she called the wedding off."

"And she did?" Rina asked, appalled.

"She wasn't that polite. She didn't even bother to tell me. She merely took off for Europe, and left me waiting at the altar." He sighed. "It taught me a valuable lesson."

"About love?"

He laughed. "Among other things. It also taught me a lot about women and their character and integrity."

Her temper flared and she narrowed her gaze on him. "Hunter, surely you can't believe that all women are like that? Without integrity, character or honor. I mean, look at your own mother.''

''Precisely,'' he said, his words chilled. Rina sighed.

''No, not your birth mother, Hunter. Your adopted mother.'' She touched his hand. ''Emma Blackwell. Surely you can't think she's without integrity, character or honor.''

''Certainly not.'' His face softened at the mention of his mother. ''Emma Blackwell is probably the most incredible woman I've ever met. Kind, loving, giving, and a woman of great honor and integrity.''

Touched by the love she could hear in his words, and see on his face, she covered his hand with hers. ''See. Your assumptions about women—lumping them all together—is not entirely valid.''

''Perhaps,'' he admitted slowly, decidedly uncomfortable talking about this. Hunter stood and began walking, obviously trying to end the conversation, but Rina wasn't about to give up now. She had a feeling this was the reason he kept withdrawing from her, kept deliberately ignoring what was happening between them.

''You've had two really rotten experiences with women. First your birth mother, and then your fiancée, but that certainly doesn't mean that all women are deceitful or without integrity. I'm certainly not,'' she added more fiercely than necessary, catching his arm to halt his movement.

Not trusting himself to look at her, Hunter sighed, looking off into the distance. ''Rina, I'd like to drop this subject for now. It's not important.'' He began walking again, obviously ending their conversation. Even though she didn't think the conversation was over—not by a long shot—she had no choice but to follow him.

''Now where are you going?'' she asked, deciding perhaps it was best not to push him on this. At least not at the moment.

''Toward the spring. We'll set up camp there tonight, use it as our base of operation.''

''Camp.'' She reached for the back of his shirt to halt him. ''What do you mean...camp?'' Tipping her head back, she glanced up at him, remembering when he confirmed her suspicions about there being some animals in the canyon. She almost shivered.

Hunter made a great pretense of glancing around. ''Well, since there doesn't appear to be a hotel in the vicinity, we'll have to make do with nature's accommodations.''

''But what about the Shaman's hogan? Can't we stay there? Surely he wouldn't mind—''

''We could,'' he acknowledged slowly. ''But my guess is that Billy's smart enough to know that by now we're looking for him, and that's the last place he'd go since he'd figure it's the first place we'd look. My guess is, he's going to make camp for the night as well, and it will be somewhere familiar to him.''

''The stream?'' His nod made her spirits sink. ''I can't wait to find that kid,'' Rina muttered.

"Neither can I," Hunter admitted with a sigh of his own.

"Yeah," Rina added, reluctantly trudging behind him and sighing heavily. "But I can't wait to find him so I can strangle him for being so blasted obnoxious."

She heard Hunter's deep, rich laugh and it caused her to smile, hoping against hope that she could change his opinion about women, show him that most women could be trusted.

Because she suddenly realized with a start, and a great deal of fear of her own, if she couldn't change his mind, if she couldn't get him to see that she could be trusted, that she had character and integrity, and that what was growing between them was something to trust, to treasure, then she was heartily afraid she was going to end up with a broken heart.

Because she knew, with a woman's instinct and a woman's fragile, frightened heart, that she was falling in love.

With a man who couldn't or wouldn't trust.

Chapter Eight

"Did you find anything?" Rina called, watching Hunter's silhouette descend toward her in the darkness.

He'd set up their makeshift camp, although Hunter's idea of a camp was a large sleeping bag and a small fire, and then he'd set off to search some more for Billy.

He'd been gone several hours now, and she'd begun feeling anxious.

And alone.

The night sounds in the canyon seemed magnified in the darkness, giving her an eerie feeling.

But she'd been too exhausted to search or walk anymore, and Hunter had suggested she stay near the stream and rest, and wait, just in case Billy showed up.

"Nope." He shook his head, closing the distance between them.

Rina shivered, curling her legs under her, wishing she'd brought her jeans with her. She'd never imagined that just this morning, when she'd pulled on a pair of shorts and a T-shirt, that by evening, she'd be chilled to the bone.

But then again, this morning, she had no idea she'd be sleeping in front of a stream, at the base of a canyon on the reservation, looking for a fourteen-year-old wayward child with more bravado than brains.

Hunter went down on his haunches in front of the fire, warming his hands.

Her gaze was drawn to those hands, so large, so perfectly sculptured, and yet so very gentle. Hands that cured, hands that soothed, hands that healed, and still had the ability to arouse her body, and more importantly, her heart.

"I've checked all the places I figured he might go," Hunter said, glancing around. "I've seen some evidence he's been here, at least in the area, but there's no recent sign of him."

"Do you think he's still in the canyon?"

The shadows of the fire danced over his features, illuminating them in a hazy, golden light. His eyes, so dark and deep, shimmered with worry, and if she wasn't mistaken, just a bit of weariness.

"I don't know for sure," Hunter said with a shake of his dark head. "It's hard to tell." With a small smile, he glanced at her, liking the way the firelight danced along her skin, warming it to a golden glow.

Her skin looked so warm, so incredibly soft, he wanted to touch it again. To touch her. But he knew he couldn't, couldn't even think about it. That was a path to sure ruin. For Billy. For The People.

And especially for him.

"But I'm about ready to agree with you," he said, forcing a smile he didn't feel. His back ached, his legs throbbed, and a tension headache was clustering behind his eyeballs. "Strangling Billy for being so obnoxious is definitely beginning to have possibilities." He was trying to make light of the situation, trying to ease the worry lines that furrowed along her brow and forehead.

He reached for his knapsack simply because he wanted to reach for her. To hold and comfort her, to ease the fears that shadowed her eyes and caused her such sadness.

With a sigh, Hunter glanced at the fire, realizing that he'd lost his peace, his sense of balance, and at the moment, he couldn't exactly pinpoint when it had happened.

Probably the moment he'd laid eyes on Rina.

He couldn't remember the last time such a thing had happened.

Yes, he could.

With Meagan.

The warning was back, loud and strong, reminding him to tread carefully.

He glanced at Rina, shadowed by the fire. She

looked small, delicate and totally defenseless. The fierce need to shield, to protect, to possess was inbred in him, culled down from generations. It was difficult resisting his natural tendencies, especially when it came to her.

"Rina," he said quietly. "Please don't worry. We'll find him. We're on the reservation. By now, everyone knows about Billy and the Shaman. Billy's not going to be able to go anywhere without being seen or recognized. He's the Shaman's grandson, a very important member of the tribe. If we don't find him, it's a good bet either Colt and his search party, or the tribal police will. He's not going to be able to run loose for long. Billy's probably cold, tired and hungry and has probably stopped to rest somewhere for the night. Someone is bound to spot him."

"And if they do?"

Hunter tried not to smile. "They will not allow him to wander off again." Of that, he was certain. Wild, wayward teenagers were a fact of life on the reservation. His own youth had been proof of that.

"You're sure?" she asked, wishing she felt as confident as he.

He laughed. "Rina, trust me. Once when I was just a bit younger than Billy, I, too, decided that the world had been unfair to me and decided to run away."

He laughed, reaching into the basket Sadie had prepared and pulling out a peach. He handed it to her, and she took it greedily, realizing she was starving.

"I made the mistake of coming into the canyon as well. Thinking everyone would be real sorry when I was missing." He laughed again, wondering now how he could have been so stupid and so naive.

"And were they?" she asked, around a mouthful of peach.

He laughed. "Actually, I was the one who was sorry. Being in the canyon during the day, or camping out with someone, especially a trusted adult at night is one thing. Being alone in the canyon when you're all alone in the dark of night is another matter."

Rina stretched her legs out and bit into her peach as the fire shifted, sending a spray of orange-glowing flames toward the inky black sky. "You got scared?"

"*Scared* isn't quite the right word for it," he said with a shake of his head. "Terrified was more like it. It's very hard to find your way around the canyon at night. The darkness is deep and echoing, as you can see. There is very little light, just a sickle from the moon to shadow your way, and of course, I didn't think far enough ahead to bring any firewood, or matches, or even any food."

"What happened?" she asked, finishing off her peach and reaching for one of the sandwiches he'd started unpacking from the square cooler pouch Sadie had stuffed with food.

"I was scared out of my mind." He shook his head as he retrieved a sandwich for himself. "I didn't realize, or I'd forgotten how cold it gets in the canyon at night. Heat rises, and when the sun sets, all the heat from the day rises, leaving the canyon cool and dark. I was exhausted, starving and terrified.''

"How'd you find your way out?"

He shook his head. "I didn't. My father went to the Shaman as soon as he discovered I was missing. The Shaman and Hallie led my dad and a search party from the reservation through the canyon. They found me at about 3:00 a.m. curled up in a ball right about in the same spot we're sitting in now.'' With a smile, he shook his head. "That's the last time I ran away, I can tell you that.''

"So, do you think this will be the last time Billy runs away?'' Her voice was wistful as she opened her sandwich and sniffed, nearly swooning at the heavenly aroma. It was some of Sadie's homemade meat loaf left over from dinner last night.

"If he's got any brains it will be.''

"He's fourteen,'' she said with a frown, taking a delicate bite of her sandwich. "I think one precludes the other.''

He chuckled, shaking his head in agreement. "How's your sandwich?'' he asked, biting into one of his own.

"Heavenly.''

"Sadie makes the best meat loaf in the world. It's what she calls comfort—'' Hunter's voice broke off when the loud shrill of his beeper pierced the air. He nearly dropped his sandwich as he searched in his pocket for his beeper. He pressed the button to reveal the number. "It's Colt."

He grabbed the knapsack and dug in it for his cellular phone, quickly punching in a number.

"Did you find him?" he asked without preamble the moment he heard his brother's voice. "Wonderful." Hunter's breath came out on a rush of relief. "They found him," he said to Rina. "And he's fine," he added, pulling her close to give her an impulsive hug.

Rina clung to him, clutching his shirt in her fists as she let her head drop to his chest in absolute relief.

"He did what?" Hunter thundered, giving his attention back to the phone and his brother.

Her head came up and she smothered a smile as he muttered something in his native tongue, something Rina was certain probably didn't need any translation.

It made her smile nonetheless.

Hunter's brows drew together, and he listened quietly for a moment, then blew out a nervous breath, his gaze searching hers.

"What's wrong?" She laid a hand to his chest, comforted by the staccato beat of his heart. It matched her own. Their eyes met.

And his mouth went dry. She was so close.

Her head was tilted up toward him, and her mouth was just a hairbreadth away. The yearning spiraled through him, blocking out the warnings that had continually clanged in his mind, warning him of the dangers of getting too involved—of losing his heart—and his objectivity about another woman.

A woman who could steal his heart, and steal one of their own from his rightful place among The People.

He had to remember that.

But he couldn't seem to prevent the overwhelming need to taste her, to brand her with his own mouth, his body, to claim her for his own.

Looking at her, holding her close to him, he wondered why he hadn't realized until now that she'd already claimed a part of his heart, carved a place for herself in his empty, lonely soul.

Dragging his gaze from hers, Hunter reluctantly forced his attention back to the phone and Colt.

"What?" He blinked, and glanced away from Rina, knowing he wouldn't be able to concentrate if he didn't. "All right. No, I understand. And you're sure Hallie will stay with him tonight?"

Still frowning, he listened, reaching out his free hand to stroke the back of Rina's hair. It was so silky. He was certain he'd never felt anything softer.

"And the Shaman?" He smiled then, knowing his brother would have checked on the old man before calling. "That's good to hear. Tell him I'll see him tomorrow."

"Anything else?" Still holding Rina close, Hunter sighed. "All right. We'll be there." He glanced around. "No, we're deep into the mouth of the canyon. It's too late and too dark for us to try to come out tonight. We'll head up at the first light of dawn. No, Colt, don't worry.'' His gaze found Rina's. "We'll be there, Colt. I promise.'' He was about to hang up, then thought better of it.

"Hey, Colt? Thanks, bro. Thank Cutter, too. All right, see you in the morning.'' He punched off the phone and tossed it one-handed to the sleeping bag, letting out a long sigh of relief.

"He's safe?'' Rina asked.

"Yeah,'' Hunter replied. He dragged his free hand over his face, letting his nerves finally calm. He hadn't realized how tense, how worried he'd been until this moment. "He's safe, Rina,'' he said, blowing out a breath and letting his gaze meet hers.

"He's safe,'' he repeated as if he couldn't quite believe it himself. He couldn't help it, he started to laugh, grabbing Rina in a celebratory hug. "Hallie Lost Souls will stay with him tonight.''

She reached up, slid her arms around his neck, and clung, letting tears of relief and gratitude fall freely, snuggling against Hunter, grateful for his presence.

There'd been so few times in her life when she'd had the comfort of another person during trying times, or happy times, that now, she didn't question and she refused to feel guilty; she merely wanted to enjoy the moment of having another to share her burden.

She couldn't stop the tears. She always cried when she was drained, exhausted, or relieved, and right now, she was all three.

Hunter felt her sobs, heard her small, silent sniffle,

and it caused something warm and soft to shift inside him. He tightened his arms around her, pulling her even tighter against him, letting the warmth and softness of her arouse his body, as her mind, her spirit had aroused his soul.

"Don't cry," he whispered, pressing his lips to her temple. She smelled of something fresh and sweet, and decidedly feminine. He was absolutely certain he'd never smelled anything sweeter, or more enticing.

Absolutely certain he'd never wanted—needed— anything or anyone more.

He fought the need, the wanting, the gut-wrenching yearning that left him feeling as tense and tangled as a randy schoolboy.

But the need and yearning were too strong, too powerful, and he'd fought them too long.

There didn't seem to be any fight left in him.

Her eyes were damp from tears and reflected the turmoil of feelings and emotions, he, too, was feeling.

Tenderly, he brushed the tangled curls from her face, then bent to kiss her eyelids, first one, then the other.

"Don't cry, please?" He let his lips trail over her face, raining a string of kisses across her face that had her arms clinging to him, and her head falling back so that the slim column of her neck tempted him.

His lips trailed down her cheeks, brushing lightly, ever so lightly at the corners of her mouth. It had her groaning, clinging to him, her fingers tangling in the dark silk of his hair.

His mouth slid down her chin, then feasted as he trailed a hot path down her neck. He paused to nibble, or to gently flick out his tongue, warming and tasting the tender skin, making her shiver, then moan in delight.

The sound seemed to feed the desire racing through him, heating his blood and hardening his body.

"Rina."

Her name came out a low groan as his hands moved up her back, pressing her even tighter against him until he felt the hardened peaks of her nipples.

He couldn't wait. He bent his head and took her mouth. Quickly. Covering her lips and pouring all the pent-up desire and longing that had been building for her and was now at a fevered pitch.

She moaned his name, then returned the kiss with the same fervor she received.

Her tongue flirted, danced, teased his, toying, tempting until he was absolutely certain he would go mad with her sweet, giving innocence.

His mouth was fervent, frantic, racing from her greedy mouth, down her neck, then lower still, moving with the purpose of a starving man finally given permission to feast on his most pleasurable desire.

He feasted.

And he savored.

He kissed her everywhere he could reach, wanting

to devour and absorb her sweet skin, wanting to brand it—and her—as his own.

Moaning softly as desire, raw and real, ripped through her, Rina pressed closer to him, wanting to ease the sudden ache that started at her center and seemed to explode and expand everywhere.

She'd never felt this…need, this frantic, desperate desire for something she couldn't express, much less understand.

Never felt this magic, these womanly feelings that made her feel alive, necessary, and more importantly, truly like a woman for perhaps the first time in her life because she knew, until this moment, she'd never really…loved. Not the way a woman should love a man.

But she loved Hunter, she knew that now. Loved all the things he was, all the things he represented, loved all the things he could be. For her. To her.

For so many years she'd felt like less of a woman simply because she'd never seemed to have these feelings that other women had. Feelings fueled by a man's touch.

Hunter had given this to her; done this to her.

And she wanted more.

Much more.

No matter what he had to offer, she wanted it, would accept it. To do any less was to deny living, loving, and worse, to deny hope.

She'd been living without love for so long, now that it was here, she could not turn her back, or her heart on it.

She realized she wanted him with all the depth and breadth of her being. Wanted him as she'd never wanted anything or anyone.

His touch inflamed her, his kisses pulsed through her, making her desperate with the need to be one with him.

"No." Hunter stopped, trying to draw away from her, fighting with himself. The warning was clanging again and he felt as if he were drowning with need, with fear. They fought a duel for control, and Hunter struggled, trying to remember what was at stake.

He was playing with fire, and too many people would get burned if he did not use caution. But his feelings for Rina were so deep, the warning was dim, drowned out by the frantic beating of his heart and the demand of his own body.

Whimpering softly, Rina pressed closer to him, rubbing her hardened nipples against his chest to bring some relief from the intense feelings that pulsed through her, unwilling to let him go.

"Hunter, please?"

He pulled her closer, ignoring the warning, hearing only her pleas. His lips raced over her again.

He bent his head, and flicked his tongue over the material of her T-shirt, before taking one extended nipple into his mouth, suckling gently, then harder, as she tangled her fingers in his hair, pulling him closer, offering herself to him in a gesture so giving, so unselfish, he nearly went weak.

She moaned. Pleasure, hot and feral raced through

her, weakening her knees and her resolve. Nothing mattered but the man in her arms and the feelings he was gently wringing from her with his clever mouth and teasing tongue.

The need to touch him, to give the same pleasure as she received ripped through her. She wanted to feel his warm skin against hers. Skin against skin in this place of nature with nothing but the stars and air between them.

Frantic, her hands roamed his wide, broad back, stroking, digging into his shoulders, feeling the heat of his skin under the cloth of his shirt.

Fingers trembling, she frantically tugged at his shirt, groaning softly as it came loose from his pants, and she could slip her hands under the material to feel the smooth, warmed skin below.

He gave a soft sigh as her warm fingers raced over his skin, touching stroking, seeking purchase.

He shifted them both, until she was lying beneath him, her long, bare legs tangled with his. With a low moan, he shoved up her T-shirt, let his lips gently touch her frantic, beating heart.

Her fingers dug into his hair as his mouth raced over her breasts, gently caressing the skin, dampening it with his tongue, teasing her nipples, letting his tongue stroke, tease, torment until she was moaning under him, wanting, begging for more.

She moaned softly as his trembling fingers fumbled with the button on her shorts. Lifting her hips to help, she tugged at his belt, then his jeans, wanting only to free him from any restraint that kept him from her.

She ran her hands over his bare, bronzed skin. It was so warm, so enticing, she couldn't resist, she let her hands seek, explore, touch until he was nearly as frantic as she.

Half crazy with desire, he heard her startled moan when his bare fingers slid the length of her long, silky thigh, then higher still. Her legs parted and she gasped when he slid one long, slender finger into her.

Hunter almost groaned aloud. She was so tight, so wet, so ready for him.

He lifted her shirt completely off to suckle her breasts, to trail his lips down the flat plane of her belly, pausing to trace her belly button with his tongue. Then his tongue traveled lower, then lower still. Her soft moans and pleas fed his desire like an accelerant and he fought for control, fought to go slow, to not frighten her. But his desire, his need for her was like a greedy living thing, begging to be fed, sated.

The first touch of his soft, clever tongue between her legs had her arching up with a loud gasp that only fed his own pleasure.

Certain she was going to explode, Rina's eyes slid closed and she let the exquisite, intense feelings drag her into a sea of pleasure that was nearly indescribable.

The climax slammed into her, hard and fast, taking her breath, her senses. Bright and beautiful colors exploded behind her eyes as an intense and glorious pleasure exploded within her body.

Fearful of losing his own control, Hunter slid his hands under her thighs, lifting her, readying her for him.

Moaning softly, Rina clung to him, pulling him closer, frantic to bridge the distance between them, to have him fill her, fulfill her, to give him the same pleasure he'd given her.

She raised her arms, tightening them around him as he knelt between her legs, pausing to smooth the hair off her face, to kiss a path where his hands had touched.

Delirium drove him, as did the soft whimpers that filled his ears as she arched up to meet him, wrapping her legs around him as frantic as he, drawing him closer, drawing him in, then deeper.

"Hunter." His name came out on a sharp breath. A jagged moan escaped her and she clung to him, fearing the world had tilted.

And she with it.

The whirlwind seemed to go on for an eternity, but didn't seem nearly long enough.

Breathing hard, driving himself deep inside her, Hunter could feel his control slowly slipping as pleasure slid along every inch of him.

When she arched up, tightening her arms and her legs around him, drawing him even deeper into her sweet, slick heat, he exploded inside her with a deep, low growl.

The ride back down to earth was slow and beautiful.

Lying beneath him, covered by his body, Rina felt safe, protected and complete. Like a lock that had finally slid home.

She had no idea how long they lay together, arms and limbs tangled, naked, enjoying the warmth and intimacy that only lovers understand.

Lovers.

She smiled, stroking a hand down his bare back. She'd never had a lover before.

Not like this.

She'd never felt anything like this. So intense, so strong, she was absolutely certain she might die of the pleasure.

With the night air cooling their heated bodies, Hunter shifted his weight. He was still buried deep inside her, and she could feel him stirring.

She moaned, shifting her hips. He groaned softly as his body responded, hardening again. He kissed her neck, letting his lips sip and soothe. Her skin was warm, and tasted sweetly of him.

"You're so beautiful. Inside. Outside." He lifted a hand and tenderly cupped her breasts, gently teasing her still-erect nipples with his thumb until she moaned softly again, her eyes sliding closed in pleasure.

With his gaze on hers, he watched the emotions cross her face as his body began a slow, gentle dance, moving within her again, until she erupted once more, calling his name and clinging to him.

With a low, strangled moan, he moved slowly this time, drawing out and enjoying the mere pleasure of feeling her body cling to his. His slow, teasing movements continued until he was certain he would go mad. He quickened his pace, thrusting harder, deeper inside her until her soft moans of pleasure filled his ears, blocking out all else as he fell over the edge and into oblivion.

After long, silent moments, he slid off her and onto his back, letting his eyes close as his heart and pulse calmed and settled.

She reached for his hand, lacing her fingers through his. He lifted her hand and kissed her fingers, slowly, one by one.

His eyes slid closed again. He was moved beyond measure by what had just happened between them.

Magic didn't come often, and when it did, it was to be savored.

He kissed her hand again.

The Apache in him understood such magic. Understood and savored it, knowing it was a special gift, one not many people received.

She tasted sweet and innocent, and she tasted of something far more important: home.

He felt it then, that inexplicable feeling of knowing he'd found that one person, the soul mate of his heart.

In the silence, the knowledge echoed like a cannon shot in his mind, bringing him to his senses.

He suddenly remembered who this woman was,

and more importantly, who he was, and what his task had been.

He remembered that he could not allow her into his life, or into his heart.

Too late.

He heard the whispered warning, as if the Spirit of Mischief were sitting on his shoulder, taunting him.

It was too late.

She'd burrowed her way into his heart.

No!

He bolted upright, rubbing his hands over his face, trying to wipe away the warning.

He could still hear it.

What had he done?

He glanced at Rina and felt his heart constrict with pain, with loss. With regret.

"No." Abruptly, he rolled to his feet, grabbing his jeans and stuffing his legs into them. "No," he said again, quickly zipping his pants.

"Hunter? What is it?" Confused, she sat up. "What's wrong?"

Stunned, she automatically reached for her T-shirt to cover herself. She was still dazed and slightly delirious from their lovemaking.

"Hunter?" Her voice held a question. In the golden light of the fire, she could see the tortured look on his face, in his eyes.

It tore at her heart.

"Hunter," she said again. She reached for him, only to have him step back from her. It came then, like the sharpened edge of a knife right to her battered, wounded heart.

"No," he said again, more forcefully this time, stepping farther away so that she wouldn't reach for him again, for he wasn't certain he could resist.

Just looking at her caused his body to ache and throb with the natural need to feel her move beneath him once again. To feel her as she took him into her body, her heart, her soul. To that place that was meant for him.

Only for him.

"We shouldn't have done this." His voice was ragged with emotion. He cursed the Spirits of Mischief for they had obviously been very busy. And he had been very foolish.

The pain of his rejection mingled with her sudden, fierce anger.

"Too late," she pointed out, pushing her hair off her face with trembling hands. "We've already done it."

"It cannot happen again."

Stunned and hurt, she merely stared at him. "It can't happen again?" she repeated, feeling her temper and anger mingle to make her voice sharp.

"No." His voice was firm, hard, detached. "This can't work. It won't work."

"Excuse me, but it seems to me it worked very well."

He dragged his shirt over his head. "It can't happen again," he said firmly.

"You mean you won't let it happen again. Because you're afraid, Hunter. Afraid because loving me, making love to me means you have to trust me, and you can't do that, can you?'' Her heart felt as if it had stopped, suspended somewhere in time.

''It doesn't matter the reason.'' He couldn't—wouldn't—admit the truth. He wouldn't admit that he wanted nothing more than to love her, to make love to her, to possess her in a way that would make her his—forever.

But it couldn't happen because he knew he couldn't allow himself to trust, to give her the power to take him into that dark, lonely abyss of pain once again, to allow himself to be vulnerable.

She'd be leaving soon, going back to her home and her life. His life was here, among his people. He would never leave, ever.

But she would, he realized. And she'd be taking his heart and his love with her.

And once again he'd be betrayed. Devastated. Desolate.

Alone.

He wouldn't go through that. Not again.

He was in grave danger. His heart, his mind, his way of life. But he'd been too caught up in his own feelings and emotions to think clearly. He couldn't allow that to happen again.

Ever.

He'd foolishly ignored the warning and walked blindly into the arms of a fiery spitfire with sad eyes and a vulnerable smile that tore at his heart.

He forced himself to look at her. And knew that

her taste, her touch would forever be branded on his heart and his soul.

For looking at her, he knew that she *was* part of his soul.

"I'm sorry, Rina. There can be nothing between us." His jaw clenched and he forced the words out. "There is no future for us. Not us. Not ever." He dragged a hand through his hair. "You have to know that."

"Why?" she demanded, feeling her heart break at his words. She refused to cry, blinking back the tears that scalded and blinded her eyes. Angrily, she brushed them away, not willing to let them fall. "Because you can't or won't trust me?"

"The reasons do not matter. This can't work."

"You don't want it to work." She had to swallow the lump in her throat to speak.

"It's not a question of what I want. It's a question of knowing what I can and cannot do." How could he explain that he wanted—needed—her more than he'd needed anything before. Needed her like fish needed water, and plants needed air. "You must forget what just happened between us," he said again with more feeling, letting his own anger and frustration lace his words. "I have."

His words speared her heart. With tears in her eyes, Rina watched him walk away from her and disappear into the darkness.

Her body felt battered, bereft, but not nearly as much as her aching heart.

Chapter Nine

Rina had no idea when he returned to camp.

Tired of waiting for him, she'd unzipped the over-size sleeping bag, and settled in, crying herself to sleep. She awoke sometime during the middle of the night when she felt something warm beside her, and realized Hunter was lying next to her. He was so warm, it was like lying next to a warmed blanket.

The fire must have died out for the dark was deep, the silence thick, echoing through the night.

If she concentrated, she could just make out the sound of his breathing, but she didn't need to hear him to know he was there.

Her body immediately reacted to his nearness, going off like a security alarm when faced with an intruder.

She lay still, quiet, staring up at the sky, trying not to think about how close he was.

But how equally far away he was.

The stars twinkled like a million brilliant dots floating above her, but she couldn't see anything for the tears blinding her eyes.

"I'm sorry." The deep timbre of his voice echoed softly through the night, startling her.

"About what?" she asked with a weary sigh. It was hard to keep the hurt, the bitterness from her voice.

"I shouldn't have let things get out of control." Lying on his back, with his arms pillowing his head, he stared up at the blackened sky. "It was wrong and I'm sorry."

She sniffled, swiping at her nose. "Great. Just what every woman wants to hear after a man makes wonderful love to her." She refused to look at him, or to hide the hurt that echoed in her voice. "He's sorry. It was wrong. That wouldn't exactly be my description of what happened between us, but hey, different strokes for different folks."

"I didn't mean to hurt you." He turned his head to look at her in the darkness. "In spite of what you may think, I do…care for you." The admission cost him, because he knew he could never tell her the truth of what was in his heart, knowing nothing could come of it. To do so would only bring heartache to both of them.

And he knew he couldn't allow himself to trust that much ever again. It was too risky, too painful, and far too frightening. The thought humbled him for he realized he hadn't been frightened of anything since he was a boy.

"The next thing I know, you're going to tell me you hope we can be friends."

"I do."

"I refuse to even dignify that with an answer." She would not let on how much he'd hurt her. Not even if it killed her. And it just might.

"We need to talk. About Billy."

She sighed. "The last time you said that to me, you told me I could never have custody of Billy. Makes a woman not want to talk to you."

He managed a smile in spite of the pain in his heart. "This is important. There's something I didn't tell you."

She sighed in the darkness, tugging the sleeping bag up tighter to her chin. She was chilled to the bone, by his words, by his coldness.

And his ridiculous stubbornness.

How could he just dismiss what had happened between them, and what they could have if only he'd get over his ridiculous fear of trusting her.

"Okay, so what do you need to tell me now?"

He sighed, knowing she wasn't going to like this little tidbit of news. "He's...uh...Billy's spending the night in jail."

"I see," she said, refusing to give in to the panic that was quickly spreading through her. Hanging on to her pride, she turned to look at him, then immediately shifted her gaze because it hurt her heart to look at him. "And exactly what did that child do to land in jail?"

"Well, when the tribal police found Billy he was...uh...hanging off one of the ledges on a bluff overlooking the canyon."

"What?" She bolted into a sitting position, stunned beyond measure at her nephew's stupidity. "What on earth was he doing hanging off a ledge of a cliff?"

He didn't answer, and she figured he was trying to spare her. At this point, she didn't mind being spared.

"I *am* going to strangle that child."

"It gets worse." He was trying not to be amused by her exasperation. In spite of what had happened between them, now that Billy was safe, nothing seemed too insurmountable.

At least not at the moment.

As long as he didn't think about his feelings for her, or his aching heart. Or what could never be between them.

Her eyes widened. "How much worse can it get?" Her gaze searched his face, then she sighed. "Never mind, I might not want to know." She took a deep breath, trying to gather her defenses. "All right, tell me the rest," she said, worried he might not.

"He was hanging off the ledge...in a car."

"In a car!" The words exploded out of her. "In a car?" she repeated incredulously, shoving her hair off her face and trying not to be frightened by the image of the danger her nephew had been in. "And where exactly did that child get a car?" she asked suspiciously, almost groaning at the look on his face. "I'm not going to like this part either, am I?"

He shook his head. "I doubt it."

"The car?" she prompted again when she didn't think he was going to tell her.

"He stole it."

"Mother of mercy," she muttered with a shake of her head. "He stole a car? Billy *stole* a car? Again?"

Hunter nodded. "He was making his way down the other side of the canyon, just as I thought. He made it far enough down to where a few small families live."

"I don't suppose he rented the car?"

"Nope."

"Bought it?"

"That would be far too practical."

She shook her head. "I can't believe that child stole a car."

Hunter's smile was grim. "He'll believe it after spending a night in jail. He stole the car on the reservation and Colt has no jurisdiction here. A couple of tribal police were in Colt's party when they found Billy. They had no choice but to take him into custody for car theft."

"But...but...that's ridiculous. Who ever heard of putting a fourteen-year-old boy—"

"Car thief," he corrected, trying not to smile at

the glare she directed at him. "A fourteen-year-old car thief, Rina."

"But they can't seriously think that Billy—"

"Stealing a car is very serious business on the reservation. Be glad it wasn't a horse," he said quietly. "Stealing a horse, why, we'd hang him for that."

That stopped her short and her mouth fell open. "You're joking?" she said frantically. "Aren't you?"

His laughter made her breath come out in a whoosh of relief.

"That's not funny, Hunter," she scolded, tempted to whack him for scaring her.

"Actually, I thought it was pretty funny."

"Cute." She shook her head. "All right. Let's have the rest of it."

"We have to be in tribal court first thing in the morning," he said, suddenly serious. "Billy has to appear before a tribal judge to answer the charges brought against him. And with the Shaman still in the hospital, the question of Billy's care and custody until the Shaman is well enough to care for him will be a matter before the court. They won't release Billy from custody until a family member stands for him, and agrees to care for him until his grandfather is well."

Her frantic gaze darted to his, as her battered heart leaped with joy. "Hunter, surely now that the Shaman has been hospitalized, and Billy has run away, the court has got to recognize that I'm the only logical choice to have custody of him. At least until his grandfather is better.''

Hope sprang to life, and she felt her dwindling spirits slowly rise. Forgetting herself, she grabbed his arm.

"The Shaman said once he is well we could discuss Billy's care. Until then, why can't I have custody? I'm his aunt, the only other family he has other than his grandfather. Surely the courts will be reasonable and recognize that these are special circumstances.''

"I can't speak for the court, Rina. I'm just a doctor. Not a tribal judge.''

"But surely they'll have to see or at least consider me as Billy's custodial guardian. At least until his grandfather is released from the hospital. They certainly can't keep Billy in jail until his grandfather is released from the hospital, can they?''

"I don't know, but it doesn't seem real practical. He is only a child.''

She frowned. "Does Billy need a lawyer? Do I need a lawyer?'' Her mind raced ahead, trying to think of every eventuality as she tried to contain her joy. "And what do I say? I've never been in court in my life. What about—''

"Whoa, whoa, whoa.'' Hunter held up his hand to stop her verbal assault. "One thing at a time, here.''

He didn't want to tell her she had no need to do anything since a tribal court would not recognize her as having any authority over Billy simply because she was not one of The People.

"Billy doesn't need a lawyer. The tribe will provide one for him. Nor do you need a lawyer, unless you plan to steal a car between now and then." His attempt at humor brought a glare from her. "Don't worry, Rina, you don't need to do anything but show up."

"But what about—" Her thoughts broke off and she dragged her hand through her hair, trying not to be alarmed. She blew out a breath. "All right. So what happens in this tribal court? And what do you think will happen to Billy because he stole a car?"

He took his time answering. "A judge will listen to the facts of the case, and take into consideration the mitigating circumstances, including the fact that Billy is the Shaman's grandson. The boy has just lost his parents. It's not uncommon that he acted out in a way that is not normal. Billy's never really been in trouble before. I'm sure the judge will take all of that into consideration."

"And then?"

"And then," Hunter said with a sigh, "he will make his ruling, and decide Billy's fate."

"Will they let me see him?"

"No," he said slowly. "Not until the hearing. Remember Rina, you're on the reservation. You're not one of The People, as such, you have no rights where Billy is concerned."

Her chin lifted. "We'll see about that," she said firmly. "First thing tomorrow morning."

* * *

"This is *not* my idea of a good time," Rina muttered to herself as she glanced around the nearly empty tribal court waiting for the proceedings to start.

She and Hunter had hiked down from the canyon just as the sun rose. The walk up was twice as bad as the hike down, leaving her winded and exhausted, not to mention just a mite testy.

They'd returned to Hunter's ranch, where they'd both quickly showered. Hunter had dropped her off at the tribal court, then headed toward the hospital to check on the Shaman.

She'd been surprised, since she'd expected him to come with her. She tried not to let it hurt that he hadn't.

She understood—she really did. His need to check on the Shaman was as important as her need to be here to stand for Billy as his only other family, but she had thought—hoped—he would be here with her if only to lend moral support and perhaps attest to her suitability as a guardian.

She'd never been in a courtroom before, never mind a tribal court.

Now, sitting here, waiting for court to convene, she felt like a fish out of water.

And she felt alone.

Totally, completely alone.

There were a few spectators sitting in the gallery alongside her, and two Native American men she assumed to be tribal lawyers sitting at the two separate tables facing the judge's bench. Several tribal police were standing around, trying to look busy and inconspicuous, to no avail.

An efficient, no-nonsense woman who repeatedly kept telling people to stay back behind the swinging gate, bustled about, shuffling through a stack of file folders, keeping an eye on the door behind the bench, a door Rina assumed the judge would come through.

When she'd arrived, the first thing she did was inquire about seeing Billy, but was politely told that she could not see him until the judge arrived and the proceedings began.

Several more people came in, filling up the rows, but Rina paid little attention to them. She was too consumed with her own worries.

She knew that Hunter believed she could not get custody of Billy because of the Indian Welfare Act, but considering the circumstances, considering that the Shaman was hospitalized, and all but incapacitated, surely they had to realize that she was the only reasonable person to care for Billy. She was his only family.

"Thought I'd come down and keep you company," Sadie said, plopping her heavy girth in the seat next to Rina and patting her hand.

Surprised, and pleased, Rina smiled at her, touched beyond measure. "I'm so grateful, Sadie, really."

"It's a scorcher out there," Sadie announced, pulling off her sun hat and fanning her face. She glared up at the ceiling where a fan slowly moved. "Wish they'd get some air-conditioning in here." She looked at Rina. "Have you seen the boy, yet?"

Rina shook her head. "No, they won't let me see him until after the proceedings." She was annoyed about the situation, but realized if she wanted any leeway with the court, and the judge, it was best not to make waves.

"Probably just as well." Sadie nodded, not in the least bit surprised. "I've raised three boys, each more wayward than the next," Sadie commented, clucking her tongue. "But none more so than Cutter. Lordy, that boy did give us some moments. Still does. What with him roaming around the world, sticking his nose in one dangerous situation after another." She sighed, fanning her face again. "It's a miracle Miz Emma ain't had a heart attack worrying about him." Sadie shook her head.

"What kind of dangerous situations?" Rina asked, curiosity suddenly getting the better of her.

"Well," Sadie began slowly, "Cutter hasn't exactly been in the military. At least not the regular military. He does what the government calls 'special assignments.' And let me tell you, it's worried his mama more than enough a time or two. You don't know Miz Emma, but she's like a mother bear with a wounded cub when it comes to her boys. Grown or not, if Miz Emma thought any of them were in trouble or danger, why, she'd go marching right after her boys, putting herself between them and any danger," Sadie said, grinning. "She's no bigger than a minute, but I wouldn't want to tangle with her. No siree, not when it comes to her boys.''

''I know the feeling,'' Rina said, realizing she felt the same way about Billy.

Sadie patted her hand. ''Now, don't you go worrying your pretty head about that nephew of yours. Miz Emma and me, we raised all three of those Blackwell men. Doesn't mean they didn't get themselves into mischief a time or two, just like Billy, but he'll straighten out. You'll see. Boys usually do.'' She chuckled, shaking her head. ''Just wish it wasn't such a headache dragging them into manhood, though.''

There was a sudden rustling in the courtroom, and then just as suddenly silence as the door behind the bench opened and a man walked in, taking his place behind the bench. He was tall, and broad shouldered with a shock of silver hair, worn in long, neat braids like the Shaman.

''That's the judge,'' Sadie whispered, reaching for Rina's hand.

A side door opened, and Billy walked in, accompanied by a tribal police officer and Hallie Lost Souls who gave her a nod of acknowledgement, and then silently took a seat in the spectators' gallery.

Seeing her nephew for the first time, Rina's heart gave a lurch and she leaped to her feet.

''Billy!'' All eyes turned toward her and for a moment, she couldn't move, she could only stare at him in absolute relief.

He seemed to have grown at least three inches

since she'd last seen him. His hair, which was as rich and black as his mother's had been, was straight, and hung nearly to his shoulders.

His eyes, which were so brown they were almost black, and almost as big as Bambi's, giving him a wide-eyed innocent look, were filled with a fear that almost broke her heart.

He wore typical teenage attire. Tattered and torn jeans that hung off his hips, and a deep green T-shirt with some inane teenage saying written on it.

Around his neck he wore a small leather pouch. It was just like Hunter's, and she had no doubt it was filled with *ha-dintin,* the pollen of tule cattails, believed by The People to protect from the Spirits of Evil. It was too bad it didn't protect teenage boys from bouts of stupidity, she thought with a sigh.

"Aunt Rina," Billy exclaimed. He stared at her in surprise for a moment, then with a strangled sob, flung his skinny body into her arms.

"Oh, Billy."

Tears filled her eyes as she held him tightly to her as he clung to her. She could feel his shoulders shake as sobs shook his slender frame.

"Don't cry, sweetheart," she crooned, stroking the back of his sleek hair, aching for his loss, his pain, his confusion.

She knew what he was feeling; she'd been just a bit older than he was now when her own parents had died.

She knew the desolation, the loss, the aching fear of being all alone in a world that wasn't accustomed to caring. She wouldn't let him stay in this world alone. No matter what the court ruled.

"Shh, sweetheart, don't cry." She rocked him in her arms, knowing the tribal judge, the tribal police as well as all the lawyers and spectators were watching, but Rina didn't care. "I know this is hard, but I'm here for you. I'll always be here for you. I love you. Do you understand?" she said as she looked into his red-rimmed eyes.

Sniffling, Billy nodded, then swiped his drippy nose with the back of his hand, shifting his feet nervously, clearly embarrassed at crying in public.

"I love you, too, Aunt Rina." He shuffled his feet again. "I'm sorry for all the trouble I caused. It's just…it's…just I miss Mom and Dad. Why did they leave me?"

In spite of his culture, in spite of the way he'd been raised, he was, in effect, still a young boy struggling to cope and understand the sudden loss of family and his sudden…aloneness.

"They didn't leave you because they wanted to," she said softly, brushing his hair off his forehead in a way she had done since he was a small child. "But sometimes these things just…happen, whether we want them to or not."

He sniffled again. "Will it ever stop hurting?" A sob broke loose even though he struggled to contain it. His narrow chest rose and fell several times in rapid succession as he tried to contain his tears. "I just want to see my dad, to talk to my mom one more time."

"I know, honey. I know." She gathered him close again, struggling not to sob herself.

She wouldn't tell him that the need to see or talk to his parents one last time would never go away. Over the years, he'd go over and over in his mind all the hurtful, careless things he'd said, and all the wonderful things he'd left unsaid.

She sighed. It was a heavy burden for any child to carry, regardless of their age, when their parents passed away, but even more so for a teenager who had no hope of understanding that life was fragile, and every moment a treasure to enjoy and savor.

Being a teenager was a painful journey at best.

"Don't cry, sweetheart. Please?" She stroked the sleek length of his hair. "Your parents loved you more than anything else in the world. That's what you need to concentrate on now." She took him by his slender shoulders and held him away from her so she could look into his eyes. "Your mother and father loved you more than anything else in this world or any other." She struggled to remember everything Hunter had taught her about the beliefs of The People. "They'll always be with you, Billy." She laid a hand on his chest. "Here in your heart. You'll always carry them and their love in your heart."

"Please be seated." The judge's voice, soft and deep, echoed through the courtroom. The tribal policeman moved to take Billy's arm, guiding him toward one of the tables in front of the judge. Billy's gaze, filled with tears and mingled with fear stayed on her, nearly breaking her heart.

She blew him a kiss, and blinking back tears, took her seat in the spectators' gallery as Billy's lawyer bent his head to speak to him.

The judge began speaking, and Rina's heart thudded wildly. "Sadie," she said, clutching the woman's arm. "I can't understand a word he's saying."

"Course not. That's cuz he's not speaking English."

Why hadn't she realized they would speak in their native tongue?

The other lawyer rose and began speaking, occasionally pointing at Billy.

Totally lost, and feeling more frantic at the moment, Rina threw caution to the wind and jumped to her feet.

"Your Honor, I'm sorry, but I can't understand a word that's being said. Could you please ask them to speak in English?"

The silence came so fast and furious, Rina blinked as all eyes in the courtroom turned to her.

The judge peered at her over the top of his spectacles.

"Young woman, who are you? And why do you ask that we speak in English? This is a tribal court."

She took a deep breath, aware that Hunter had slipped in the back door, and had taken a seat and was now watching the proceedings.

She swallowed hard, lacing her hands together in front of her to keep them from trembling.

"I'm well aware that this is a tribal court, Your Honor. And I don't mean any disrespect, truly I don't. But I'm Billy's aunt. His late father's sister, and other than his grandfather, I'm Billy's only relative. His welfare is of great concern to me." She took a deep breath for courage, realizing she was shaking. "It is imperative that I understand what is going on."

The judge looked at her for a long moment, nearly making her squirm. "You realize young woman that even if you are the boy's aunt you have no authority in this courtroom. This is a *tribal* court," he found it necessary to point out again.

"Yes, Your Honor, I understand." She wasn't going to back down, not on this. It was too important.

The judge stared at her long and hard, and then finally sighed, glancing down at the manila folder on the bench.

"All right," he said, obviously taking pity on her. "For this morning, we will speak in English," he instructed, letting his gaze take in all the participants before bringing his gaze back to hers. "Even though this *is* a tribal court." He directed his gaze to Billy's lawyer. "You may proceed."

Billy's lawyer rose. "Your Honor, Billy has been charged with car theft, and we don't deny the charges. He did indeed steal a car—"

"Is that true, young man?" the judge inquired, glaring at Billy.

"Yes, Your Honor," Billy muttered, hanging his head.

"Obviously you have not heeded the teachings of your elders," the judge commented sadly. "You have brought shame to your grandfather, young man. And to your tribe and your people. You are aware of that?"

"Yes, Your Honor." Billy's head was still hanging so his words sounded garbled and muttered.

"And are you also aware that stealing is not only a crime, but not the way of *Tin-ne-åh?*"

"Yes, sir," came the mumbled reply.

"Young man." The judge paused, waiting for Billy to look up at him. "You must learn that one cannot run from pain. It is a natural part of this great life. I am not without some understanding in this matter. I am well aware that your parents have left this place, to become one with the universe, but even though they may not be here in body—" the judge placed a hand on his heart "—they are always here. In spirit." His features softened into a smile. "Always remember that, son." The judge glanced around, pushing his glasses up as he inspected Billy's file.

"Now, since this is your first offense, and considering the unusual circumstances, and your special place in the tribe, I am willing to grant you leniency, providing you abide by several conditions."

"Yes, Your Honor."

"Please stand up, Billy," the judge ordered, and Rina tensed as he glanced around. "Is there a representative from the boy's family here to stand for him?''

Rina jumped to her feet again. ''Your Honor, I told you, I'm the boy's aunt, and his family representative.''

Once again all eyes turned toward her and the judge sighed.

''And as I've told you, young lady, this is a tribal court and even though you are the boy's aunt, you have no authority in my courtroom.''

Dismissing her, he glanced around again. ''Is there a representative from the boy's family present?'' Pointedly, he glared at Rina. ''His *tribal* family,'' he clarified, lest there be any mistake.

Refusing to be dismissed, Rina clenched her fists at her sides, trying to hang on to her temper.

''Your Honor, like it or not, I *am* the boy's family. His only family. And now that his grandfather is ill, and in the hospital, surely you can see that he's not capable of caring for the boy, or having custody of him. I'm more than willing and able to care for the boy.'' She had to swallow. ''I'd like you to grant custody of Billy to me at least until his grandfather is out of the hospital and he and I can discuss the matter further.''

She planned to reason with the Shaman, pleading if necessary. Surely a man as wise as he was reported to be would realize that he couldn't care for Billy. Not in his physical condition. It would be detrimental to both of them.

The judge turned to her, leveling her with a dark gaze.

"Young lady, are you saying you don't believe the Shaman is capable of caring for his grandson?" The disbelief in his voice echoed around the room.

She wanted to roll her eyes, for Hunter had said the same thing to her on more than one occasion.

Aware that all eyes were once again on her, Rina swallowed hard, banking down her frustration.

"It's not that I don't think he's capable of caring for his grandson," she said carefully. "But he's ill and aged—"

"There is wisdom and respect in age," the judge interrupted. "We believe that our elders are our greatest resource, something to be treasured and revered, not dismissed and scorned, something I'm sure you do not understand." The judge shifted the file in front of him. "What is your name, young woman?"

"Rina." Smoothing her hair back, she glanced around self-consciously. "Rina Roberts."

The judge nodded. "Ms. Roberts, please try to understand. Although your intentions are honorable, and I do not doubt your love for the boy, you have no rights in this courtroom, or any rights to your nephew. He is a Native American child, more importantly, he is the grandson of the Shaman. As such, he holds a sacred place among The People. It is up to me to make sure that he fulfills the destiny granted to him by the Spirits." The judge paused. "Now, any legal matters, whether of custody or any other matter regarding the boy are to be handled and settled by this court. All decisions handed down by me are legally binding. Do you understand that?''

She nodded. ''Yes, but—''

''Sit down, Ms. Roberts,'' the judge ordered in a voice that brooked no argument. ''The matter of Billy Eaglefeather's care and custody is not your concern.''

Desperate, Rina refused to sit. ''But Your Honor, surely you have to see that—''

''Sit!'' he ordered, banging his gavel and nearly making her jump out of her shoes.

Sadie tugged Rina's hand. ''Come on now, honey, sit down. It won't do any good to tick the man off.''

''Your Honor.'' Hunter was on his feet, making his way toward the front of the courtroom, and Rina glanced back at him gratefully.

Surely Hunter would be able to tell the court that she was reliable, responsible and more than capable of caring for Billy, at least until his grandfather was out of the hospital. Who else was going to care for Billy? Surely, they couldn't keep him in jail?

''May I speak to the court?'' Hunter asked respectfully.

''Ahh, Dr. Blackwell,'' the judge acknowledged with an affectionate smile. ''It is good to see you again. I understand you had occasion to see my grandson the other day.''

Hunter smiled, pushing through the swinging gate

that separated the judge from the spectators. "Yes, Your Honor. And how is Joey?"

The judge chuckled. "Under house arrest on his mother's orders so that he does not get into any further mischief. At least not this week." His brows drew together thoughtfully. "The child is my joy, but he does have an adventurous spirit. Takes after his grandmother, I'm sure," he said, chuckling softly. "So what brings you before the court this morning, Dr. Blackwell?"

"I am here on behalf of the Shaman, as Billy's family representative."

"Ahh, I see." Smiling, the judge leaned back in his chair, clearly pleased. "And how is the Wise One?"

Hunter spoke carefully. "Doing better, Your Honor. I believe he will be released from the hospital within a week, two at best. Until then, I ask, on behalf of the Shaman, and on behalf of The People that you grant custody of Billy to me."

"Wait a minute!" Stunned, Rina jumped to her feet again, ignoring Sadie who was tugging on her hand again. Anger raced through her and she glared at Hunter, wondering what the heck he was doing. "He can't have custody of Billy, he's not even a relative."

"I *am* the boy's godfather," Hunter countered, speaking to the judge and deliberately not looking at Rina. "And a member of The People."

Rina's mouth dropped open in shock and she

glared at Hunter, stung by his betrayal. How could he ask for custody of her nephew?

How could he do this to her when he knew how important it was to her?

Accepting that custody might go to Billy's grandfather was one thing.

Accepting that Hunter had deliberately betrayed her by asking for custody himself was quite another.

If he hadn't come forward, perhaps she would have had a chance to get custody, at least temporarily, until the Shaman was well, and that was all she'd hoped for, time to talk to Billy's grandfather, to reason with him. She hoped he understood and loved Billy enough to do what was best for him.

Billy had already lost one set of parents; with his grandfather's health in the state it was, it wasn't fair to set the boy up to lose another.

Rina was relatively young and very healthy, and planned on being around for a long, long time—at least long enough to raise Billy to adulthood, just as she had done for her brother James.

"Dr. Blackwell's...not even related to the boy," she stammered again, trying not to cry. "How can he ask for custody? That's the most ridiculous thing I've ever heard."

"Oh, boy," Sadie muttered under her breath as everyone looked at Rina again.

"Young woman," the judge began slowly, shifting his gaze from Hunter to her. "I understand that you are distraught due to the recent death of your brother, and the circumstances surrounding your nephew's arrest. However, do not for a moment think that I will continue to put up with this nonsense.'' He took a deep breath, templed his fingers, and began speaking slowly—as if she were an addled child.

"I want you to listen and understand what I'm saying. Billy is a member of The People. With his parents' deaths, his custody automatically goes to his grandfather on behalf of his mother's tribe. In the event that his grandfather is unable to care for the boy, then care and custody of Billy will be granted to another responsible elder of the tribe. Billy is one of the last descendants of the Teyas, so it is my right and responsibility to make certain he is brought up correctly—''

"I can bring him up correctly,'' she argued, letting tears of anger and frustration fill her eyes.

The judge shook his head, then looked at her kindly. "And tell me, Ms. Roberts, what do you know of the Teyas, or the Holy-Life Way of The People?''

"I—I'm learning,'' she stammered, glancing wildly at Hunter who hadn't spared her a glance since he'd made his request of the judge. "Ask Dr. Blackwell.''

The judge glanced at Hunter, but chose not to speak to him, instead, directing his attention back to Rina again.

"Indeed,'' he said thoughtfully. "You probably are learning some of our ways, customs and traditions. But it is not the same as growing up knowing your place in the tribe. Tell me, when the boy is grown and the Love Spirit chooses a mate for him, do you know how to proceed, do you know how to instruct your nephew in the ways of The People? Or how to impart the wisdom he will need to fulfill his destiny?"

Frantically, her mind raced backward, wishing she'd paid more attention when she was at Mary's, weaving the marriage basket. But since Mary hadn't spoken but a few words in English, Rina hadn't been able to understand her, let alone remember what the woman had said.

"Your Honor, please. Maybe I don't know everything I need to know, yet. But I'm willing to learn."

The gavel banged loudly again. "This matter is settled." He turned to Hunter. "On behalf of The People, and the Shaman, Dr. Hunter Blackwell will be granted temporary custody of this young minor child, Billy Eaglefeather, until such time as his grandfather, the Shaman, is well enough to care for him. At such time, custody will once again revert to his grandfather. As for the matter of the theft of the vehicle—" the judge swiveled in his chair and directed his gaze to Billy, who was still standing "—young man you will make restitution to the family you took the car from by working for them for the rest of the summer, a minimum of four hours per day every day as a form of community service."

"Yes, Your Honor," Billy mumbled, head down.

"Speak up, child. I'm old and partially deaf. I

can't hear when you talk to your shoes," the judge said.

"Yes, sir," Billy said, lifting his head and his voice so that it rang through the courtroom.

"Son, it is important that you learn the consequences of your actions. For every action, there is a reaction. What that reaction is will depend on the actions you take. I want you to spend the next four months thinking of that."

"Yes, sir."

The judge smiled. "And if you do not get into any more trouble during the next four months, Billy, and I trust that you won't, and if you fulfill your obligations of community service, the charges will be dismissed. Do you understand and agree?"

"Yes, Your Honor."

"Fine. Please remember everything you do reflects on your family, your people, and especially your grandfather. You have a responsibility to him, and to The People to make them proud. Do you understand?"

Billy nodded.

"I'm sorry son, I can't hear you."

"Yes, sir."

"Good. Good." The judge smiled, closing the manila file in front of him. "Now, you will be returned to your cell until all the paperwork is completed and your release officially secured." The judge glanced at Hunter. "You can return this afternoon to pick the boy up, Dr. Blackwell. Case dismissed." The gavel banged and the judge rose.

"Wait!" Rina cried. "Can I see Billy?"

The judge turned and looked at Hunter. "Dr. Blackwell, it is up to you. The boy's welfare is in your hands."

Hunter turned to Rina. He could see the pain, the accusations in her eyes, and knew that she felt as if he'd betrayed her.

He hadn't betrayed her; he merely had done what he'd promised the Shaman. He had explained the situation to her as best he could. He had protected Billy, and The People.

But in doing so, he realized sadly, he had hurt the woman he loved.

"Hunter." Her voice was husky with emotion. "Please?" She hated the pleading tone of her voice, hated the pain that radiated from her heart to every fiber of her being.

"Rina, I have no wish to keep you from Billy." His eyes pleaded with her to understand.

"You could have fooled me." She took a step closer, trying to control the hysteria, the pain his actions had caused. "All this time, Hunter, all this time, I kept wondering what to do, how to get you to trust me enough to accept what was between us." She sniffled, swiping at her nose. "It never occurred to me that I was the one who should have been worried about trusting—you." Her words tore at his heart. "You deliberately betrayed me. Set me up to trust you by pretending to help me learn the ways of The People, all the while knowing that you were going to ask for custody of Billy." She blinked away tears. "And you talk about women's character and integrity? You ought to look in the mirror." She whirled away from him, wanting only to go someplace so she could be alone and cry her heart out.

"Rina, wait." He went after her, catching her arm. "That's not true. That's not how it was." She shrugged off his arm, ignoring him. "Rina, wait. Please." He held on tight so she had no choice but to stop. "You've got it all wrong. Let me explain."

"There's nothing to explain. I understand perfectly." She lifted her chin. "Are you going to let me see Billy?" There was a challenge in her voice as she struggled to hold on to her pride.

"Of course," he said in exasperation, dragging a hand through his hair. He had to get her to listen to reason, to understand he had no choice. He had to do what he'd done. To honor his commitment to the Shaman, The People. But from the look on her face he knew she wasn't ready to accept or listen to what he had to say. Hopefully, in a few days she'd calm down enough for him to explain, but he feared if he didn't do something fast, he might not have those few days. "Billy will be staying with me until the Shaman is released from the hospital. Why don't you stay, too, so you can have some time with Billy?"

Swallowing past the lump in her heart, she turned, her heart aching at the sight of him.

As much as she detested the thought of having to impose upon Hunter or his hospitality any further, especially now, she had no choice.

She wanted to see Billy, to spend time with him, and she couldn't afford to stay in a hotel for a week, nor could she afford to rent a car to get back and forth. She had no choice but to accept his offer. Like it or not.

"Thank you," she said stiffly. "I appreciate your generous offer and I'll try not to be a bother."

He moved closer, unable to bear the look on her face, in her eyes, knowing he'd put that look there.

"Rina, please. You would never be a bother." How could he tell her what was in his heart? The feelings, the knowledge that seared deep, permanently.

He went to reach for her, but she shrunk back from him. "I didn't do this to hurt you," he said softly.

"Oh, really?" One brow rose and she fought back her tears. "If you had another purpose, forgive me, I can't see it. You knew how much this meant to me. Knew how much I wanted, needed custody of Billy, and this was my only chance. How could you ask the judge to give you custody?" She needed to understand why he'd done such a thing; why he'd deliberately hurt and betray her.

"You've known all along that the chances of your getting custody were negligible—no, almost impossible. I've always been honest with you about that."

"I am Billy's only blood relative. I had a better than even chance until you announced you wanted custody."

He looked at her long and hard. "You had no chance."

"Why couldn't you let me find that out for myself? Or at least let me try without asking for custody? You took away my only chance."

Her lips trembled as tears threatened again. She was absolutely certain her heart was breaking in two, from betrayal, from loss. She wasn't certain she couldn't take anymore. "You know I'm capable of caring for and raising Billy."

"No," he said slowly, deliberately making his voice gentle. "I really don't know any such thing. You're not one of The People, Rina, no matter how much you refuse to acknowledge it. You are a white woman, and a white woman raising a half-breed child in a world that cannot accept him can be a dangerous thing."

She scowled, swiping at her tears. "No, Hunter, I don't agree." She took a step closer. "But I'll tell you what I do know. Trust supposedly means so much to you, and yet you can't give it. But when someone gives you their trust, you think nothing of betraying it."

"No, it wasn't like that at all." He reached for her again but she shrunk back. "I didn't mean to hurt you."

"I'm sorry, but I'm afraid I don't believe you."

"Rina, please."

She shrugged off his hand. "Please don't touch me," she said quietly, knowing if he did, she would cave in. And she couldn't. The pain, the sorrow, the loss was too deep. "We have nothing further to say."

He couldn't bear to let her just walk away from him. "Rina, please, wait. Let me explain."

She stopped, turning to him. "Why? Have you changed your mind? Are you going to let me have custody of Billy until the Shaman is well again?"

He shook his head. "I can't do that."

Blinking back tears, she lifted her chin. "I'll stay with you Hunter, for Billy's sake, and selfishly for my own sake until the Shaman is well and I can speak to him directly about Billy's care. But don't— don't make the mistake of thinking I will ever trust you again."

"Rina, wait, please don't say—"

"You've deliberately betrayed me, and right now all I want is to be with my nephew."

"But what about...what about...us?"

She looked at him long and hard. Twenty-four hours ago his words would have sent her heart soaring. Now, they only made her feel more desolate.

"There is no 'us,' Hunter. You said so yourself. Well, you've gotten your wish." With that, Rina turned and fled the courtroom.

Chapter Ten

"Dr. Blackwell?" Beth Anne said, standing in the door of the examining room as Hunter comforted a cranky toddler who'd taken great umbrage at the DPT inoculation he'd just given to her.

Hugging the child close, Hunter soothed the baby, turning his attention to his nurse. "Yes, Beth Anne?"

"The hospital just called. They said your... your..." She was stumbling over words again, and wringing her hands. "Your...grandfather can come home this afternoon."

"Thank you, Beth Anne," he said, nodding. For the first time in two weeks Hunter smiled. This news pleased him as nothing else had the past few weeks. Since he'd been granted temporary custody of Billy, he'd been absolutely, utterly miserable.

Not because of Billy, but because of Rina.

Even though she'd been staying in the house, she barely spoke to him unless it was to discuss or tell him something about Billy's care.

Even Sadie was being curt with him, he thought with a sigh as he reached for a sugarless lollipop to give to the crying toddler.

In all the years he'd known Sadie, he'd never known her to get mad at him. At any of the brothers.

Well, he realized, she was always getting mad at one of them, but she'd never stayed mad. Not like this.

He'd been so miserable, the ache in his heart so deep, he began to wonder if he'd made a mistake about Rina.

Once again the words she'd hurled at him that morning in court replayed in his mind over and over again, leaving an ache in his heart.

After passing the toddler back to his mother, he washed his hands, then headed down the hall toward his private office.

He'd always tried to be an honorable man, to live his life to make both his adopted fathers—Justin and the Shaman—proud of him.

But he wasn't certain now if he was proud of himself.

He had done the right thing, the only thing he could, he told himself. But was it? he wondered as he slumped in his desk chair to stare blindly out the window.

He'd hurt Rina, and in her mind betrayed her.

Absently, he glanced at the framed picture of his family on his desk. His mother, small and delicate, beaming up at his father, his brothers.

His father, tall and strong with his arm protectively around his mother, his eyes filled with love for her and for his sons.

He could see them all: Colt and Cutter, and then of course, himself. He stood out because he was different, but he'd never felt different, he realized, never felt different because his parents had loved and accepted them all equally. They'd loved him because of who he was, not because of what he was.

Right from the beginning, they'd trusted him enough to take him into their home, their hearts.

Even knowing it was a risk.

He'd never thought he was the kind of man who was afraid of risk.

Until he'd met Rina and realized loving her might be the biggest risk of all.

Had he been wrong all this time about her? About them? About himself?

Had he merely been blind? Holding on to his own fears and frustrations, using them as a way to protect himself from getting hurt again.

The possibility brought a bright, searing hope to his heart, and he picked up the phone to make a long-distance call.

He wasn't sure what to do, but he knew someone who would. He smiled, then leaned back in his chair, cradling the phone between his ear and shoulder. His smile widened, and his heart filled when the phone was answered. His gaze drifted to the photo once again and he reverently touched it.

"Mom," he said with a smile. "How are you?" His eyes slid closed as he leaned back in his chair. "Yeah, I love and miss you, too."

"Hallie, have you heard any more about the Shaman's condition?" Rina asked, as she watched Hallie Lost Souls quietly rock on the porch rocker.

Since she hadn't spoken to Hunter during the past two weeks since the tribal court hearing, Hallie Lost Souls had been coming by each day to continue to teach her about the Holy-Life Ways.

In spite of her own personal misery over the situation with Hunter, she'd grown to care for Hallie deeply. He was kind, gentle and generous with his time, but he was not so generous with his words, and not exactly a fountain of information.

He had a tendency to answer questions with a word or two that almost invariably left her more curious or lost than before she'd asked.

"Yes." He continued to slowly rock, staring off into the distance. "I have heard."

She bit back a smile. "Do you think you could tell me what you have heard?"

"His health is better."

"That's wonderful," she said, truly relieved. "Do you have any idea when he might be released from the hospital?"

Hallie's rocker squeaked softly. "Two days ago."

Hope flared anew. The sooner Rina could talk to

the Shaman personally, the sooner she was certain they could straighten this matter out. She frowned suddenly as his words registered.

"You mean in two days he'll be released?"

"No," Hallie said, continuing to rock.

"No?" She frowned, shaking her head. "I don't understand."

"The Shaman was released from the hospital two days ago."

"What!" Her own rocker abruptly stopped. "What do you mean?"

Hallie continued to rock, frowning now. "Two days ago, the Shaman returned to his hogan." His frown deepened. "Now do you understand?"

"Yes," she said, shaking her head. "No."

Hallie thought he'd better try again. He spoke slowly and deliberately. "Two days before this day—"

"No, no, no, Hallie," she said with a laugh, laying a gentle hand on his arm. "I understood what you said. I just...just didn't believe it."

His rocker stopped midrock and he turned to her, his eyes wide and sad. "I would not speak lies to you, Rina Roberts. You are my friend." He looked so hurt, she patted his arm.

"No, no, no, Hallie, I believe you." She smiled to reassure him. "Honest." What she couldn't believe was that the Shaman was home, and Hunter just happened to forget to mention it.

He knew she was waiting to speak to the Shaman personally.

The knowledge that he'd kept this from her was just like another dagger, another betrayal in her heart.

She jumped to her feet. "Hallie?"

"Yes."

"Will you take me to see the Shaman?"

"Yes." He didn't move.

"Now?" she specified, lest he thought she meant sometime in the distant future.

"Yes, I will take you now," he said with a slow nod of his head.

"The woman who needs a good meal is here to see you," Hallie whispered in the Shaman's ear.

The Shaman was sitting with a shawl wrapped around his shoulders, propped up in a chair in the living room of his home.

It was basically two large rooms with a thatched roof. One room served as a combination kitchen-living room, and through a doorway she assumed was a bedroom.

An older woman busied herself in the kitchen, cooking something that smelled heavenly, while a floppy eared beagle sat at the Shaman's feet.

"She needs to speak to you of your grandson," Hallie whispered.

The Shaman nodded, motioning Rina inside. She'd stood in the open doorway, waiting for Hallie to announce her.

Hesitantly, she stepped over the threshold, not certain what to expect.

"Come and sit with me." The Shaman motioned her forward, a smile on his face, in his eyes. "I understand you have been helping to care for my grandson," he said as Rina sat down in the old wooden rocker facing him.

"Yes," she said hesitantly, glancing at Hallie, grateful he had stayed. He had moved behind the chair where the Shaman sat and was now quietly watching them.

"He is a good boy, and will be a fine man." The Shaman managed a chuckle, in spite of his slightly labored breathing. "Once he outgrows his…spirited youthfulness."

"Youthfulness." Rina tried not to smile as she rolled the word around on her tongue, thinking that car theft and hanging off ledges might qualify as a bit more than spirited youthfulness. "Well, that's one way of looking at it."

"Perhaps the penguins have the right idea about youth, no?" The Shaman's eyes twinkled as her mouth fell open.

"How…how…" Her gaze darted to Hallie's and she wondered how the Shaman knew of the penguin story she'd told Hunter.

He chuckled. "It is an old Indian folklore, passed on from father to spirited youthful son. Unfortunately, time has lost part of the story."

Fascinated, she learned forward, resting her elbows on her knees. "Please, tell me the rest of the story."

He adjusted the shawl around his shoulders with slightly trembling hands.

"It is said that the Spirit of Wisdom will show a man how to be a man. But first, he must go off on his own, relying only on himself, letting his youthful spirit run free, in order to accept and understand the seriousness of what it means to be a man."

He paused thoughtfully, taking a slow, deep breath. "It is not until a man is free of this youthful spirit that he can learn to care for himself, and it is not until he can care for himself, that he can learn to care for others and the universe around him. It is not until this time that he can find his inner peace, the harmony that will guide him in the Holy-Life Way of The People." He nodded, smiling gently at her.

He was talking of Billy, she knew, but she was thinking of Hunter, and how troubled he'd been, by her and what had happened between them, by what happened to Billy, by the Shaman's illness.

Her love for him was enough that she wanted him to be happy, to find his peace if that's what he needed to make him happy.

"But what if a man cannot find that peace?" she asked with a frown.

"Ah, if a man cannot find his peace it is merely because he is not listening." He laid a hand on his chest. "A man must learn to listen with his ears, but also with his heart."

Touched, she smiled at him. "Hunter was right, you are very wise."

He chuckled. "And very old, but there is wisdom in age, just as there is spirit in youth. Each has their place." He reached down to scratch the dog behind the ears, his eyes never leaving hers. "I understand how you feel about the boy," he said quietly. "For he is a part of us both."

"Yes."

"But do you understand his sacred place in the tribe?" He looked at her kindly, his eyes wise, and knowledgeable. "More importantly, do you understand the tribe's sacred place in the boy's heart?" He sighed, lacing his fingers together to rest on his stomach. "I have a duty to The People to teach the boy all that I know. I am old now, my time growing short. It is important that my grandson be prepared to take his sacred place among The People. My place," he clarified, making Rina's eyes widen.

"Billy will take your place?" The news came as a shock, but perhaps now she understood why Hunter had been so adamant about Billy growing up on the reservation. "As the Shaman?"

"Yes," he admitted with another smile. "I was not blessed with a son, only a daughter whom I loved well. But only the males of the tribe inherit powers." He shrugged, his eyes twinkling mischievously. "The spirits have not yet gotten into equality, I think."

She laughed at his joke.

"Billy has not yet received his powers, but perhaps it is for the best, considering his youthful...spiritedness. He must be wise enough and mature enough to use his powers and his wisdom wisely." His gaze, soft, kind, knowledgeable found hers. "Do you understand?"

"Yes," she said softly, finally understanding so much more.

"Let me ask you a question."

"Of course, anything."

The Shaman held out one frail, wrinkled hand to her. She took it, and moved closer to sit at his feet.

"You love the boy, as do I. I can see it in your eyes, in your heart. Like your brother before you, you are a wise and good person."

Tears blurred her vision. Knowing that the Shaman approved of James was very important to her. "Thank you."

"The boy, he is the best of us, is he not?" the Shaman asked, his gaze searching hers.

"Absolutely." And it was true, she realized.

"He is a part of both of us, both of our cultures. I do not want to deny him the benefit of your culture, nor do I want him to be denied the benefit of mine." The Shaman sighed. "We are adults, blessed with more wisdom—"

"And less...spiritedness," she added with a smile, making him chuckle.

"Yes, well there is that," he said with a nod. "And I think we have the opportunity to give Billy the best of both of our cultures, to know and learn about each because he is a part of each." He took a slow, deep breath, waving away a cup of tea Hallie held out to him.

"In order to fulfill the destiny of his manhood, I believe Billy needs the benefit of both of us. He will need my wisdom and knowledge of The People in order to walk among them, to live among them. But he will also need the love and gentle touch of a mother's strong hand and heart."

Her heart soared, feeling hope. "What…what do you propose?"

"You are a teacher, are you not? Sharing your own wisdom and knowledge with the young, like your brother?"

"Yes, I am," she said, frowning. "But I don't exactly have a job at the moment." She shrugged, looking sheepish.

"I see." He was quiet for a moment. "Would you like to continue to teach?"

"Absolutely."

"You know, we are not so very different. You share your knowledge and wisdom with others as do I."

Anxious, Rina leaned forward, tightening her hand on his. "Shaman, what is it you want me to do?"

"No, it is not what I want. It is what is best for you and for the boy." He lifted his hand and laid it on her head. "I propose that we give Billy the best of us, the best of our cultures, our wisdom, our worlds."

"You mean share him?"

"In a manner of speaking." He sighed. "With your brother's death, The People were left without a teacher. It is still not so easy to get teachers to come here. We are a poor tribe, and not many feel the rewards are worth the sacrifices.''

"I couldn't care less about money. What I care about is being able to be part of Billy's life.''

He smiled, pleased by her answer. "Then Rina, would you be willing to share Billy? To move to the reservation—we will provide a house of course—and to teach your wisdom and knowledge to our young? In doing so, you will be a major part of Billy's life. He can spend his time with both of us, learning the best of both of his cultures.''

Her gaze searched his. "Are you saying…are you saying you'd let Billy stay with me sometime? In my house? On the reservation?''

He laughed, patting her head the way a grandfather would do. "Of course. How else can he learn the ways of your people?''

"So you're saying if I move here, to the reservation, we can raise Billy together?''

"Yes.'' His gaze found hers. "I think it is the best solution for all, but especially for the boy.''

Touched, she rose to her feet. "I can do this,'' she said, feeling like she wanted to jump for joy. "I can really do this.'' She bent and kissed his weathered cheek, unable to contain her excitement, her joy. "Hunter was right. You are a wise man.''

He laughed. "Let us hope the boy learns some of that wisdom—our wisdom—'' he corrected with a grin ''—as well.'' He struggled to his feet, pushing the blanket off his lap, and letting Hallie help him to his feet.

"Come now, let us drink tea and eat fry bread." He took her arm to steady himself, his steps slow and halting. "Before the good doctor comes to yell about my diet." Eyes twinkling, he led Rina into the kitchen.

"Aunt Rina, are you kidding?" Throwing himself against her, Billy hugged her tight. "You're really staying here, on the rez?"

Laughing, she hugged him back, praying the kid wasn't going to damage her ribs by hugging her so tight.

"Yes, I'm staying." She released him and leaned back on the railing of the front porch. She'd spent the rest of the afternoon and early evening with the Shaman, then Hallie had brought her back to Hunter's ranch after dinner. This was the first opportunity she'd had to speak to Billy, since he'd been doing his community service all afternoon. "I'm going to teach."

"Just like Dad," he said with awe, his eyes shining with joy. "I'm glad. This is gonna be awesome."

"Awesome, huh?" She tilted her head thoughtfully. "You know what this means don't you?"

He frowned, wondering if he'd missed something. "What?" His frown deepened at her smile. "What?"

"It means young man, that you're going to have

to mind your p's and q's and behave. You're going to have to answer not just to your grandfather, but to me as well.''

Billy considered it for a moment, then grinned. "Cool. How soon are you going to move? Grandpa said I can come home anytime now that he's out of the hospital." Billy scratched a mosquito bite. "I like Hunter's house and all, but Aunt Rina, I gotta tell you, Sadie makes me eat broccoli.'' He scowled. "I hate broccoli."

"It's good for you," Sadie said, opening the front door and walking onto the porch, her hands filled with a tray of lemonade and a plate of brownies. "Makes you grow strong and handsome." She winked at Rina. "Like Hunter, Colt and Cutter.''

Billy considered that for a moment, then grinned. "I could handle that."

"Have a brownie," Sadie said, offering the tray. "You're still growing, kid, better have two.''

Munching on a brownie, Billy asked Rina, "When you gonna move?"

"I was thinking about tomorrow," she said, trying to ignore the fact that Hunter's truck was pulling into the driveway. She'd done her best to avoid him the past few weeks.

He'd made his decision, and she knew there was no hope, not for her, not for them. He couldn't trust, and she couldn't love a man who thought so little of the trust she gave him.

It hurt, deeply, a hurt she was certain would never

heal. But she had to accept it and go on, in spite of the hurt, because to do anything less would be futile.

"Billy, I'm going to go upstairs to start packing. Please tell your uncle I'll be leaving in the morning." She stood as well, knowing she wouldn't be able to see Hunter, not without having her heart break just a little more.

It would be easier to leave if she didn't have to see him.

"Sure," he said, bouncing off the porch. "I'll tell him."

"And tell him…goodbye," she whispered, before turning and heading into the house before anyone could see her tears.

The door to her bedroom flew open and Rina jumped. She'd been standing by her bed, folding clothes to pack into her suitcase.

"So you're leaving?" Fists clenched, Hunter stood in the doorway, a thunderous look on his face. He glared at her suitcase lying open on the bed.

He hadn't bothered to ask questions. The moment Billy had told him his aunt was upstairs packing, he knew he had to do something. Anything. He couldn't let her go. Fear had propelled him up the stairs and to her bedroom door.

"Yes," she said, turning to face him.

"Just like that, you're leaving." He shook his head, unable to believe it. All that he'd feared for so long had materialized. He'd fallen in love with her, and now she was leaving him. He wasn't certain he could bear it. Wasn't certain he could accept life without her.

"And you wondered why I couldn't trust you. I knew you'd leave eventually." Taking his heart with her.

"Don't you dare—dare talk to me about trust!" Rina exclaimed, storming up to him. "How dare you!" She whacked him in the chest. He didn't budge. She whacked him again. "How dare you say something like that after the viscous, vile thing you did to me?" Tears of fury and frustration glinted in her eyes as she glared up at him. "I trusted you. You're the one who betrayed me."

"No." He shook his head, unable to bear the truth. "I did what I had to do for The People, for Billy, for the Shaman."

"You did what you did for yourself, Hunter. Don't blame this on anyone else. You could have told me what you had planned that night in the canyon, but you didn't, you preferred to let me go on thinking I might have a chance of custody."

"I couldn't tell you that night."

"And why not?"

"Because," he yelled, frustration propelling his words. " I...I couldn't think of anything that night, except you." He reached for her. "Please, don't leave."

"Give me a reason to stay," she challenged, but he just stood there looking at her. Furious, she poked him again. "For an educated man, you're an idiot."

His mouth snapped closed and he merely stared at her—glared at her.

She gave him a poke in his chest, just to make sure he was still listening. She wasn't about to explain that she wasn't really leaving, but in effect staying. That wouldn't change the fact that he didn't trust her enough to allow himself to love her, that they had no future together. Hadn't he told her so?

"And you've got your nerve," she fumed. "I'm doing exactly what you've wanted me to do all along. Exactly what you've told me to do. I'm doing what's best for Billy. Isn't that what you wanted?"

"I don't know what the hell I want," he yelled. "Except you." He reached for her, but she stepped back. "I want you, Rina."

"You want me, as long as it doesn't require loving or trusting, and I can't and won't accept that. It's not enough. I deserve more. Now, please go away and leave me alone." Trying to control her tears, she gave his chest a push, and shut the door in his face, leaving him standing there with his mouth open.

Something woke her up.

Rina groaned. It wasn't enough that she'd cried herself to sleep, and given herself a headache, now she was having a nightmare.

Accompanied by very bad music.

Her eyes fluttered open and she groaned, realizing she couldn't be having a nightmare since she was awake.

She groaned again in the darkness as the music intensified.

Well, she supposed Billy thought it was music.

She had no doubt he'd fallen asleep with his radio on again. The sound was...earsplitting. Off-key enough to make her teeth hurt.

She sat up, pushing her hair off her face, and the sheet off her legs. She was about to climb out of bed to go shut the kid's radio off when she heard a gentle knocking at her bedroom door.

"Who is it?" she asked.

"Aunt Rina?" Billy's voice was hushed. "Could you open the door a minute?"

And could you turn off your music, she wanted to ask, but didn't. Instead, she climbed out of bed and went to open the door.

Billy was leaning against the doorjamb, eating an orange.

"Hi," he said with a big grin, biting into the orange with gusto.

One brow rose. "Hi?" She glanced around him. "Billy, what are you doing?" she asked suspiciously, hoping he wasn't about to drop another round of spirited youthfulness on her.

"Eating an orange," he said, grinning wider.

She rolled her eyes. "Obviously you've been taking speech lessons from Hallie Lost Souls," she muttered under her breath. "All right, you're eating an orange." She nodded her sleepy head to let him know she'd at least gotten that part. "Now, do you want to tell me why you're standing in my doorway, in the middle of the night, eating an orange, while your radio is playing that awful racket that's masquerading as music?''

''My radio's not on. And I'm eating an orange because Uncle Hunter gave it to me.''

She blinked at him, then held up her hand. ''Excuse me, one thing at a time. First the music. If your radio isn't on, then where is that racket coming from?''

''The yard.''

''The yard?'' she repeated suspiciously.

He pointed toward her bedroom window. ''Go look.''

He followed her to the window. She looked out, but couldn't see anything.

''Open the window, Aunt Rina.''

''Why?'' She was just tired enough to be suspicious. ''Is a bucket of water or something going to fall on me?''

He laughed. ''Nope. Just open it.''

She opened it. The music got louder. Off-key, barely discernible, but definitely louder. She looked down.

''What in the world...''

Hunter was standing in the yard, right below her window, playing a...flute.

Badly.

''Are you crazy?''

''Look what he brought for me, Aunt Rina.'' Billy showed her the marriage basket, the one she'd made the morning at Mary's. It was wobbly and lopsided, and not in the least bit attractive, but to her it was the most beautiful sight in the world.

Her mouth fell open.

It was overflowing with an assortment of apples, oranges, pears, nuts and plastic-wrapped packages of microwave popcorn. No doubt Hunter's modern-day version of corn.

She remembered him telling her the story about when the Love Spirit picked a mate for a man, there was a ritual that went along with the courtship. The gifts, the flute playing, asking the family for a woman's hand.

"He's asked for your hand in marriage." Billy grinned, obviously enjoying himself.

"He what!"

"Asked for your hand in marriage," Billy repeated, rooting through the basket for another piece of fruit. She laid a hand on his to stop him.

"No more fruit until you tell me what's going on." The music continued, so she leaned out the window. "Hunter, Sadie's going to call the cops if you don't stop that racket."

"That's real nice," he commented, looking up at her with a smile that warmed her through and through. "I come to play you the marriage song and you call it racket."

Billy leaned past her to look out the window. "Uncle Hunter, what are you going to pledge for my aunt's hand in marriage?" he said, grinning.

She hit Billy gently on the arm. "Will you two stop talking about me like I'm not here."

"Aunt Rina," Billy said. "I have a solemn duty as the only male in your family to make certain you make a good match." He let a grin slip loose, thrilled to be taken in Hunter's confidence, and even more thrilled to know that his aunt and his uncle, were going to be his aunt and his uncle—through marriage—if all went according to plan.

With a sigh, she let him lean out the window again.

"Okay, Uncle Hunter, what's it going to be?" Billy laughed. "And you'd better make it good." He glanced affectionately at his aunt. "She's worth a lot."

"I was going to offer a pony, but I know that as the man in the family, you'd probably much prefer this little red 1967 Camaro I've got my eye on. Once you turn sixteen," Hunter added, just to make sure he didn't contribute to any more spirited youthfulness.

"A 1967 Camaro!" Delighted, Billy almost fell out the window in his desire to high-five the air. Rina grabbed him by the back of his shirt and hauled him inside.

"Then I have your permission to marry your aunt?" Hunter called.

Billy shrugged, grabbing an apple and taking a big bite. "Fine by me." He grinned. "I'm getting a car out of the deal."

Scowling, Rina leaned out the window. "Don't you think I might have a say in this? I don't want to marry you, Hunter. I won't marry a man who can't trust me enough to love me.''

"I love you.'' Hunter swiped his hand down his jeans, more nervous than he realized. His heart was in his mouth, and he realized he was scared to the bone. He swallowed because his throat was suddenly dry, making it hard to speak. "And I...trust you.'' His gaze searched hers. "I'm sorry I hurt you, sorry if you felt I betrayed you. I didn't see it that way. I just saw it as doing something for Billy, The People and the Shaman. But now I can see that you must have thought—felt it was a betrayal. And I'm sorry.''

The sincerity of his voice had her throat constricting.

"I love you, Rina," he called. "With all my heart. I want to make a future with you. A family. To grow old with you.'' He took a step closer to the window, his palms sweating. "I'm asking you to forgive me, to love me, to live with me and love with me for the rest of our days.''

"What about the nights?'' she questioned, her heart soaring.

"Them, too," he assured her.

She frowned down at him, pretending to consider. "Are you ever going to play that blasted flute again?''

He laughed, tucking it in his back pocket. "Not ever.'' He looked up, but she was gone. His heart panicked and he glanced around.

He took a step back, just in time to see a small

redheaded bundle, dressed in a white cotton gown, come barreling barefoot down the steps.

"I love you," Rina said, launching herself into his arms, and planting kisses all over his face.

"I love you, Rina," he whispered, kissing her hard on the mouth, holding her, loving her, feeling whole for the first time in his life.

"I love you, too," she whispered, searching his gaze. "Are you sure? I don't want you to have any doubts or fears."

He shook his head. "I'm sure. I've waited for you my whole life, Rina. I realize that now. Trusting someone is part of loving them. They're a package. You can't have one without the other. And by the time I realized I did trust you, I also realized I loved you." He shrugged. "So I'm a little slow. An educated idiot as some would say." He kissed her, holding her tight, loving her. "You made me believe it."

"Oh, Hunter."

"It's about time you got on with it, bro," Colt said, leaning out a bedroom window to enjoy the goings-on.

"You can say that again," Cutter agreed, leaning out of his own window.

"Thought I was going to have to box that boy's ears to put some sense into him," Sadie added, leaning out her own window with a smile.

"I'm coming down," Billy announced to the crowd in general. He raced down the steps, nearly tripping on his laces in his hurry.

"Hey, Uncle Hunter, Aunt Rina? When are you

getting married? And exactly how soon can I get my car?''

With a laugh, Rina and Hunter grabbed Billy, enfolding him in their embrace as love flowed between them, blending them together until their hearts were one.

Hunter's gaze met Rina's. ''I love you,'' he whispered, knowing the words, the feelings were true, and real.

''I love you, too.''

Epilogue

Six months later

"Hunter," Rina whispered softly, turning in his arms to plant a kiss along his jaw. "How...how do you feel about...children?"

He laughed, shifting his weight so that she lay under him, protecting her with his body. "I'm a pediatrician, remember?" He nuzzled her neck, savoring the scent of her, a scent he could never get enough of. "You'd better hope I love children," he added with a laugh, stringing kisses down her neck to her collarbone.

"Yes," she said hesitantly. "I know, but I mean how do you feel about having your...own children? Our children?"

He lifted his head to look at her, his eyes questioning.

They were lying naked under the stars, in front of the lake, near the Shaman's summer hogan. It was their six-month anniversary and this seemed the perfect place to celebrate their love; the place where they had first shared their love.

"Rina, what do you mean?" His gaze searched hers, realizing her eyes were shining with what the Shaman would have called a "woman's mystery."

"I thought…the doctors said you can't conceive."

"Yes, that's what they said, but they also said they couldn't find any medical reason for it."

"Sometimes, hon, these things just happen. There's no medical explanation for it. But that doesn't affect my love for you." He kissed her to reassure her.

"But would you…like a child of our own?"

He sighed, measuring his words, knowing how careless words had almost cost him the most important thing in his life: her.

"Yes, I would like a child of our own, but it's not a requirement, Rina. We have Billy, and each other, and the family, and more than enough love to go around."

With a grin, she looped her arms around his neck, trying to hide her smile. "Mary and the Shaman have put their heads together."

"And?" he asked with a lift of his brow.

"And they think that since traditional medicine hasn't helped me conceive, and since there is no medical reason for it, then perhaps it's time for a little...tribal medicine."

"I see," Hunter said. He had lived too long with the Shaman's ways not to believe in his powers.

"But before I do...anything, I want to be certain how you feel about having a child." Her gaze found his. "Our child. A child that would be part of you and part of me," she added carefully.

He knew what she was asking, questioning, and it hurt his heart to know that she would still have worries after all this time.

"Rina. Oh, Rina," he said, touching her cheek. "You want to know how I'll feel about a child that will be a half-breed, right?"

Chewing her lower lip, she nodded. She'd been so afraid to bring this up for fear she might hurt him, but she had to know.

"Rina," Hunter began slowly. "When I fell in love with you, I realized how wrong I had been. How ridiculous my opinions were, but they were based on my own experiences, my own pain." He brushed the hair off her face, kissing her gently. "Falling in love with you, and having you love me in return taught me that it doesn't matter what culture a child comes from. What matters is the love that surrounds that child, and we have more than enough love to go around."

"Oh, Hunter." Lifting her hands, she cradled his face, bringing it close for a kiss. She loved him so much. "I want your child—our child more than anything in the world."

"Then maybe the Love Spirit will bless us again," he said with a smile, leaning down to kiss her, gently at first, then taking them deeper until all thought ceased and only feelings and love existed. "And if he doesn't we still and always will have each other."

* * * * *

Look for Sharon De Vita's next book,
THE MARRIAGE PROMISE, book two of
THE BLACKWELL BROTHERS *series,*
on sale in March 2000,
only from Silhouette Special Edition.

A Letter from the Author

Dear Readers,

I've often wondered what really makes a family. Is it birth and bloodlines? Or is it love and shared memories? Well, I think it's a little of both. All of us have friends that we can claim are "just like family." And since families are the heart of what keeps us all going, I wanted to explore the dynamics of another family in my new miniseries: The Blackwell Brothers.

Now, these men aren't brothers by birth or blood, but by love and memories. Each had been adopted as a young boy by Emma and Justin Blackwell, a couple with an abundance of love and no one to give it to.

Now, there's nothing I like better than writing about men, especially, strong, handsome, stubborn men—with hearts of gold. The Blackwell Brothers are all three with a little mischief thrown in, of course.

The first book, *THE MARRIAGE BASKET,* is about Hunter Blackwell. Hunter tries to straddle two worlds: the white man's world, and the Native American world. He's been fortunate because his adopted father, Justin Blackwell, encourages him to nurture the cultural ties of his heritage, and it's because of these cultural ties that Hunter Blackwell falls in love.

As the tribal and the Blackwell town's pediatrician, Hunter becomes embroiled in a custody battle for another child—his godson—when the boy's parents are killed in a car accident. But Rina Roberts, the boy's aunt, has other ideas about who should raise Billy, a young boy who, like Hunter, was born to one white parent and one Native American parent, a boy destined, like Hunter, to handle two worlds.

Although Rina and Hunter have their differences, both cultural and parental, about who is best to care for Billy, they both learn that love—unconditional love—for a man, a woman and a child can bridge all barriers no matter what they are. And families aren't just bound by blood ties, but also by love ties. So come along with me on a new adventure, to the small town of Blackwell, Texas, and meet three of the sexiest men alive. In the coming months you'll meet Cutter Blackwell, and Colt Blackwell, as each learns about the true meaning of family, and love.

Sharon De Vita

If you enjoyed what you just read,
then we've got an offer you can't resist!

Take 2 bestselling love stories FREE!

Plus get a FREE surprise gift!

SILHOUETTE'S 20ᵀᴴ ANNIVERSARY CONTEST
OFFICIAL RULES
NO PURCHASE NECESSARY TO ENTER

1. To enter, follow directions published in the offer to which you are responding. Contest begins 1/1/00 and ends on 8/24/00 (the "Promotion Period"). Method of entry may vary. Mailed entries must be postmarked by 8/24/00, and received by 8/31/00.

2. During the Promotion Period, the Contest may be presented via the Internet. Entry via the Internet may be restricted to residents of certain geographic areas that are disclosed on the Web site. To enter via the Internet, if you are a resident of a geographic area in which Internet entry is permissible, follow the directions displayed on-line, including typing your essay of 100 words or fewer telling us "Where In The World Your Love Will Come Alive." On-line entries must be received by 11:59 p.m. Eastern Standard time on 8/24/00. Limit one e-mail entry per person, household and e-mail address per day, per presentation. If you are a resident of a geographic area in which entry via the Internet is permissible, you may, in lieu of submitting an entry on-line, enter by mail, by hand-printing your name, address, telephone number and contest number/name on an 8"x 11" plain piece of paper and telling us in 100 words or fewer "Where In The World Your Love Will Come Alive," and mailing via first-class mail to: Silhouette 20ᵗʰ Anniversary Contest, (in the U.S.) P.O. Box 9069, Buffalo, NY 14269-9069; (In Canada) P.O. Box 637, Fort Erie, Ontario, Canada L2A 5X3. Limit one 8"x 11" mailed entry per person, household and e-mail address per day. On-line and/or 8"x 11" mailed entries received from persons residing in geographic areas in which Internet entry is not permissible will be disqualified. No liability is assumed for lost, late, incomplete, inaccurate, nondelivered or misdirected mail, or misdirected e-mail, for technical, hardware or software failures of any kind, lost or unavailable network connection, or failed, incomplete, garbled or delayed computer transmission or any human error which may occur in the receipt or processing of the entries in the contest.

3. Essays will be judged by a panel of members of the Silhouette editorial and marketing staff based on the following criteria:

   Sincerity (believability, credibility)—50%
   Originality (freshness, creativity)—30%
   Aptness (appropriateness to contest ideas)—20%

   Purchase or acceptance of a product offer does not improve your chances of winning. In the event of a tie, duplicate prizes will be awarded.

4. All entries become the property of Harlequin Enterprises Ltd., and will not be returned. Winner will be determined no later than 10/31/00 and will be notified by mail. Grand Prize winner will be required to sign and return Affidavit of Eligibility within 15 days of receipt of notification. Noncompliance within the time period may result in disqualification and an alternative winner may be selected. All municipal, provincial, federal, state and local laws and regulations apply. Contest open only to residents of the U.S. and Canada who are 18 years of age or older, and is void wherever prohibited by law. Internet entry is restricted solely to residents of those geographical areas in which Internet entry is permissible. Employees of Torstar Corp., their affiliates, agents and members of their immediate families are not eligible. Taxes on the prizes are the sole responsibility of winners. Entry and acceptance of any prize offered constitutes permission to use winner's name, photograph or other likeness for the purposes of advertising, trade and promotion on behalf of Torstar Corp. without further compensation to the winner, unless prohibited by law. Torstar Corp and D.L. Blair, Inc., their parents, affiliates and subsidiaries, are not responsible for errors in printing or electronic presentation of contest or entries. In the event of printing or other errors which may result in unintended prize values or duplication of prizes, all affected contest materials or entries shall be null and void. If for any reason the Internet portion of the contest is not capable of running as planned, including infection by computer virus, bugs, tampering, unauthorized intervention, fraud, technical failures, or any other causes beyond the control of Torstar Corp. which corrupt or affect the administration, secrecy, fairness, integrity or proper conduct of the contest, Torstar Corp. reserves the right, at its sole discretion, to disqualify any individual who tampers with the entry process and to cancel, terminate, modify or suspend the contest or the Internet portion thereof. In the event of a dispute regarding an on-line entry, the entry will be deemed submitted by the authorized holder of the e-mail account submitted at the time of entry. Authorized account holder is defined as the natural person who is assigned to an e-mail address by an Internet access provider, on-line service provider or other organization that is responsible for arranging e-mail address for the domain associated with the submitted e-mail address.

5. Prizes: Grand Prize—a $10,000 vacation to anywhere in the world. Travelers (at least one must be 18 years of age or older) or parent or guardian if one traveler is a minor, must sign and return a Release of Liability prior to departure. Travel must be completed by December 31, 2001, and is subject to space and accommodations availability. Two hundred (200) Second Prizes—a two-book limited edition autographed collector set from one of the Silhouette Anniversary authors: Nora Roberts, Diana Palmer, Linda Howard or Annette Broadrick (value $10.00 each set). All prizes are valued in U.S. dollars.

6. For a list of winners (available after 10/31/00), send a self-addressed, stamped envelope to: Harlequin Silhouette 20ᵗʰ Anniversary Winners, P.O. Box 4200, Blair, NE 68009-4200.

Contest sponsored by Torstar Corp., P.O. Box 9042, Buffalo, NY 14269-9042.

PS20RULES

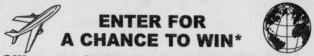

ENTER FOR
A CHANCE TO WIN*

Silhouette's 20th Anniversary Contest

Tell Us Where in the World
You Would Like *Your* Love To Come Alive...
And We'll Send the Lucky Winner There!

Silhouette wants to take you wherever
your happy ending can come true.

Here's how to enter: Tell us, in 100 words or less,
where you want to go to make your love come alive!

In addition to the grand prize, there will be 200
runner-up prizes, collector's-edition book sets
autographed by one of the Silhouette anniversary
authors: **Nora Roberts, Diana Palmer,
Linda Howard** or **Annette Broadrick**.

DON'T MISS YOUR CHANCE TO WIN!
ENTER NOW! No Purchase Necessary

Silhouette®
Where love comes alive™

Name: _____

Address: _____

City: _____ State/Province: _____

Zip/Postal Code: _____

Mail to Harlequin Books: **In the U.S.**: P.O. Box 9069, Buffalo, NY
14269-9069; **In Canada**: P.O. Box 637, Fort Erie, Ontario, L4A 5X3

*No purchase necessary—for contest details send a self-addressed stamped envelope to:
Silhouette's 20th Anniversary Contest, P.O. Box 9069, Buffalo, NY, 14269-9069 (include
contest name on self-addressed envelope). Residents of Washington and Vermont may
omit postage. Open to Cdn. (excluding Quebec) and U.S. residents who are 18 or over.
Void where prohibited. Contest ends August 31, 2000.

PS20CON_R